MARJORIE DEAN HIGH S
FRESHMAN

BY

PAULINE LESTER

MARJORIE DEAN, HIGH SCHOOL FRESHMAN

CHAPTER I

THE PARTING OF THE WAYS

"What am I going to do without you, Marjorie?" Mary Raymond's blue eyes looked suspiciously misty as she solemnly regarded her chum.

"What am I going to do without you, you mean," corrected Marjorie Dean, with a wistful smile. "Please, please don't let's talk of it. I simply can't bear it."

"One, two—only two more weeks now," sighed Mary. "You'll surely write to me, Marjorie?"

"Of course, silly girl," returned Marjorie, patting her friend's arm affectionately. "I'll write at least once a week."

Marjorie Dean's merry face looked unusually sober as she walked down the corridor beside Mary and into the locker room of the Franklin High School. The two friends put on their wraps almost in silence. The majority of the girl students of the big city high school had passed out some little time before. Marjorie had lingered for a last talk with Miss Fielding, who taught English and was the idol of the school, while Mary had hung about outside the classroom to wait for her chum. It seemed to Mary that the greatest sorrow of her sixteen years had come. Marjorie, her sworn ally and confidante, was going away for good and all.

When, six years before, a brown-eyed little girl of nine, with long golden-brown curls, had moved into the house next door to the Raymonds, Mary had lost no time in making her acquaintance. They had begun with shy little nods and smiles, which soon developed into doorstep confidences. Within two weeks Mary, whose eyes were very blue, and whose short yellow curls reminded one of the golden petals of a daffodil, had become Marjorie's adorer and slave. She it was who had escorted Marjorie to the Lincoln Grammar School and seen her triumphantly through her first week there. She had thrilled with unselfish pride to see how quickly the other little girls of the school had succumbed to Marjorie's charm. She had felt a most delightful sense of pardonable vanity when, as the year progressed, Marjorie had preferred her above all the others. She had clung to Mary, even though Alice Lawton, who rode to school every day in a shining limousine, had tried her utmost to be best friends with the brown-eyed little girl whose pretty face and lovable personality had soon made her the pet of the school.

Year after year Mary and Marjorie had lived side by side and kept their childish faith. But now, here they were, just beginning their freshman year in Franklin High School, to which they had so long looked forward, and about to be separated; for Marjorie's father had been made manager of the northern branch of his employer's business and Marjorie was going to live in the little city of Sanford. Instead of being a freshman in dear old Franklin, she was to enter the freshman class in Sanford High School, where she didn't know a solitary girl, and where she was sure she would be too unhappy for words.

During the first days which had followed the dismaying news that Marjorie Dean was going to leave Franklin High School and go hundreds of miles away, the two friends had talked of little else. There was so much to be said, yet now that their parting was but two weeks off they felt the weight of the coming separation bearing heavily upon them. Both young faces wore expressions of deepest gloom as they walked slowly down the steps of the school building and traversed the short space of stone walk that led to the street.

It was Marjorie who broke the silence.

"No other girl can ever be as dear to me as you are. You know that, don't you, Mary?"

Mary nodded mutely. Her blue eyes had filled with a sudden rush of hot tears.

"But it won't do any good," continued Marjorie, slowly, "for us to mourn over being separated. We know how we feel about each other, and that's going to be a whole lot of comfort to us after—I'm gone." Her girlish treble faltered slightly. Then she threw her arm across Mary's shoulder and said with forced steadiness of tone: "I'm not going to be a silly and cry. This is one of those 'vicissitudes' of life that Professor Taylor was talking about in chapel yesterday. We must be very brave. We'll write lots of letters and visit each other during vacation, and perhaps, some day I'll come back here to live."

"Of course you will. You must come back," nodded Mary, her face brightening at the prospect of a future reunion, even though remote.

"Can't you come with me to dinner?" coaxed Marjorie, as they paused at the corner where they were accustomed to wait for their respective street cars. "You know, you are one of mother's exceptions. I never have to give notice before bringing you home."

"Not to-night. I'm going out this evening," returned Mary, vaguely. "I must hurry home."

"Where are you going?" asked Marjorie, curiously. "You never said a word about it this morning."

"Oh, didn't I? Well, I'm going out with——Here comes your car, Marjorie. You'd better hurry home, too."

"Why?" Marjorie's brown eyes looked their reproach. "Do you want to get rid of me, Mary? I've oceans of time before dinner. You know we never have it until half-past six. Never mind, I'll take this car. Good-bye."

With a proud little nod of her head, Marjorie climbed the steps of the car which had now stopped at their corner, without giving her friend an opportunity for reply. Mary looked after the moving car with a rueful smile that changed to one of glee. Her eyes danced. "She hasn't the least idea of what's going to happen," thought the little fluffy-haired girl. "Won't she be surprised? Now that she's gone, Clark and Ethel and Seldon ought to be here."

A shrill whistle farther up the street caused her to glance quickly in the direction of the sound. Two young men were hurrying toward her, their boyish faces alight with enthusiasm and good nature.

"It's all O.K., Mary," called the taller of the two, his black eyes glowing. "Every last thing has been thought of. Ethel has the pin. She'll be along in a minute."

"It's a peach!" shouted the smaller lad, waving his cap, then jamming it down on his thick, fair hair. "We've been waiting up the street for Marjorie to take her car. Thought she'd never start."

"I am afraid I hurt her feelings," deplored Mary. "I forgot myself and told her she'd better hurry home. She looked at me in the most reproachful way."

"Cheer up," laughed Clark Grayson, the black-eyed youth. "To-night'll fix things. All the fellows are coming."

"So are all the girls," returned Mary, happily. "I do wish Ethel would hurry. I'm so anxious to see the pin. I know Marjorie will love it. Oh, here comes Ethel now."

Ethel Duval, a tall, slender girl of sixteen, with earnest, gray-blue eyes and wavy, flaxen hair, joined the trio with: "I'm so glad we waited. I wanted you to see the pin, Mary." She was fumbling busily in her shopping bag as she spoke. "Here it is." She held up a small, square package, which, when divested of its white paper wrapping, disclosed a blue plush box. A second later Mary was exclaiming over the dainty beauty of the bit of jewelry lying securely on its white satin bed. The pin was fashioned in the form of a golden butterfly, the body of which was set with tiny pearls.

"Oh-h-h!" breathed Mary. "Isn't it wonderful! But do you suppose her mother will allow her to accept such an expensive gift? It must have cost a lot of money."

"Fifteen dollars," announced Clark, cheerfully, "but it was a case of only fifty cents apiece, and besides, it's for Marjorie. Fifteen times fifteen dollars wouldn't be too much for her. Every fellow and girl that was invited accepted the invitation and handed over the tax. To make things sure, Ethel went round to see Marjorie's mother about it and won her over to our side. So that's settled."

"It's perfectly lovely," sighed Mary in rapture, "and you boys have worked so hard to make the whole affair a gorgeous success. I'm afraid we had better be moving on, though. It won't be long now until half-past seven. I do hope everyone will be on time."

"They've all been warned," declared Seldon Ames. "Good-bye, then, until to-night." The two boys raised their caps and swung down the street, while Mary and Ethel stopped for one more look at the precious pin that in later days was to mean far more to their schoolmate, Marjorie Dean, than they had ever dreamed.

CHAPTER II

GOOD-BYE, MARJORIE DEAN

"Whatever you do, don't laugh, or speak above a whisper, or fall up the steps, or do anything else that will give us away before we're ready," lectured Clark Grayson to the little crowd of happy-faced boys and girls who were gathered round him on the corner above Marjorie Dean's home. "We'd better advance by fives. Seldon, you go with the first lot. When I give the signal, this way," Clark puckered his lips and emitted a soft whistle, "ring the bell."

"Right-o," softly retorted three or four boyish voices.

Clark rapidly divided his little squad of thirty into fives, and moved toward the house with the first division. Two minutes later the next five conspirators began to move, and in an incredibly short space of time the surprise party was overflowing the Dean veranda and front steps. The boy who had been appointed bell ringer pressed his finger firmly against the electric bell. There came the sound of a quick footstep, then Marjorie herself opened the door, to be greeted with a merry shout of "Surprise! Surprise!"

"Why—what—who!" she gasped.

"Just exactly," agreed Clark Grayson. "'Why—what—who'—and enough others to make thirty. Of course, if you don't want us——"

"Stop teasing me, Clark, until I get over my surprise, at least," begged Marjorie. "No, I never suspected a single thing," she said, in answer to Ethel Duval's question. "Here are mother and father. They know more about all this than they'll say. They made me believe they were going to a party."

"And so we are," declared her father, as he and Mrs. Dean came forward to welcome their young guests, with the cordiality and graciousness for which they were noted among Marjorie's friends.

"Come this way, girls," invited Marjorie's mother, who, in an evening frock of white silk, looked almost as young as the bevy of pretty girls that followed her. "Mr. Dean will look after you, boys."

Once she had helped her mother usher the girls into the upstairs sleeping room set aside for their use, Marjorie lost no time in slipping over to the dressing table where Mary stood, patting her fluffy hair and lamenting because it would not stay smooth.

"You dear thing," whispered Marjorie, slipping her arm about her chum. "I'll forgive you for not telling me where you were going. I was terribly hurt for a minute, though. You know we've never had secrets from each other."

"And we never will," declared Mary, firmly. "Promise me, Marjorie, that you'll always tell me things; that is, when they're not someone else's secrets."

"I will," promised Marjorie, solemnly. "We'll write our secrets to each other instead of telling them. Now I must leave you for a minute and see if everyone is having a good time. We'll have another comfy old talk later."

To Mary Raymond fell the altogether agreeable task of keeping Marjorie away from the dining-room, where Mrs. Dean, Ethel Duval and two of her classmates busied themselves with the decorating of the two long tables. By ten o'clock all was ready for the guests. In the middle of each table, rising from a centerpiece of ferns, was a green silk pennant, bearing the figures — embroidered in scarlet. The staffs of the two pennants were wound with green and scarlet ribazine which extended in long streamers to each place, and was tied to dainty hand-painted pennant-shaped cards, on which appeared the names of the guests. Laid beside the place cards were funny little favors, which had been gleefully chosen with a sly view toward exploiting every one's pet hobby, while at either end of each table were tall vases of red roses, which seemed to nod their fragrant approval of the merry-making.

"It's quite perfect, isn't it?" sighed Ethel, with deep satisfaction, gently touching one of the red roses. "The very nicest part of it all is that you've been just as enthusiastic as we over the party." She turned affectionate eyes upon Mrs. Dean.

"It could hardly be otherwise, my dear," returned Mrs. Dean. "Remember, it is for my little girl that you have planned all this happiness. Nothing can please me more than the thought that Marjorie has so many friends. I only hope she will be equally fortunate in her new home, though, I am sure, she will never forget her Franklin High School chums."

"We won't give her that chance," nodded Ethel, emphatically. "There, I think we are ready. Clark wants to be your partner, Mrs. Dean, and Seldon is to escort Marjorie to her place. We aren't going to give her the pin until we are ready to drink the toasts. Robert Barrett is to be toastmaster. Will you go first and announce supper?"

There was a buzz of delight and admiration from the guests, as headed by Marjorie and Seldon, the little procession marched into the dining-room. For a moment the very sight of the gayly decked table with its weight of goodies and wonderful red roses caused Marjorie's brown eyes to blur. Then, as Seldon bowed her to the head of one of the tables, she winked back her tears, and nodding gayly to the eager faces turned toward her and said with her prettiest smile: "It's the very nicest surprise that ever happened to me, and I hope you will all have a perfectly splendid time to-night."

"Three cheers for Marjorie Dean! May we give them, Mrs. Dean?" called Robert Barrett.

Mrs. Dean's smiling assent was lost in the volume of sound that went up from thirty lusty young throats.

"Now, Franklin High," proposed Mary Hammond, and the Franklin yell was given by the girls. The boys, who were nearly all students at the La Fayette High School, just around the corner from Franklin, responded with their yell, and the merry little company began hunting their places and seating themselves at the tables.

Marjorie was far too much excited to eat. Her glances strayed continually down the long tables to the cheery faces of her schoolmates. It seemed almost too wonderful that her friends should care so much about her.

"Marjorie Dean, stop dreaming and eat your supper," commanded Mary, who had been covertly watching her friend. "Clark, you are sitting next to her. Make her eat her chicken salad. It's perfectly delicious."

"Will you eat your salad or must I exercise my stern authority?" began Clark, drawing down his face until he exactly resembled a certain roundly disliked teacher of mathematics in the boys' high school. There was a laugh of recognition from the boys sitting nearest to Clark. He continued to eye Marjorie severely.

"Of course, I'm going to eat my salad," declared Marjorie, stoutly. "You must give me time, though. I'm still too surprised to be hungry."

But the greatest surprise was still in store for her. When everyone had finished eating, Robert Barrett began his duties as toastmaster. Ethel Duval came first with "What Friendships Mean to a Schoolgirl," and Seldon Ames followed with a ridiculously funny little toast to "The High School Fellows." Then Mr. and Mrs. Dean were toasted, and Lillian Hale, a next-door neighbor and the only upper-class girl invited, gave solemn counsel and advice to the "freshman babies."

As Marjorie's dearest friend, to Mary had been accorded the honor of giving the farewell toast, "Aufwiedersehen," and the presentation of the pin. Mary's clear voice trembled slightly as she began the little speech which she had composed and learned for the occasion. Then her faltering tones gathered strength, and before she realized that she was actually making a speech, she had reached the most important part of it and was saying, "We wish you to keep and wear this remembrance of our good will throughout your school life in Sanford. We hope you will make new friends, and we ask only that you won't forget the old."

"I can't begin to tell you how much I thank you all," Marjorie responded, her tones not quite steady, her face lighted with a fond pride that lay very near to tears. "I shall love my butterfly all my life, and never forget that you gave it to me. I am going to call it my talisman, and I am sure it will bring me good luck."

But neither the givers nor Marjorie Dean could possibly guess that, in the days to come, the beautiful golden butterfly was to prove anything but a talisman to the popular little freshman.

CHAPTER III

THE GIRL WHO LOOKED LIKE MARY

"It's rather nice to have so much room, but I know I shall never feel quite at home here," murmured Marjorie Dean, under her breath, as she came slowly down the steps of her new home and paused for a moment in the middle of the stone walk which led to the street. Her wistful glance strayed over the stretch of lawn, still green, then turned to rest on the house, a comfortable three-story structure of wood, painted dark green, with lighter green trimmings. Her mother's sudden appearance at the window caused Marjorie to retrace her steps. Luncheon was ready.

"Everything is so different," she sighed, as she climbed the steps she had so lately descended. "I've been here a week, and I haven't met a single girl. I don't believe there are any girls in this neighborhood. I should feel a good deal worse, too, if the Franklin girls hadn't been such dears!" Marjorie's last comment, spoken half aloud, referred to the numerous letters she had received since her arrival in the town of Sanford from her Franklin High School friends, now so many miles away. Mary Raymond had not only fulfilled her promise to write one long letter every week, but had mailed Marjorie, almost daily, hurriedly-written little notes full of the news of what went on among the boys and girls she had left behind.

It had been a busy, yet a very long week for Marjorie. The unpacking of the Deans' furniture, which had been shipped to Sanford a week before their arrival there, and the setting to rights of her new home had so occupied the attention of Mrs. Dean and Nora, her faithful maid-of-all-work, that Marjorie, aside from certain tasks allotted to her to perform, was left for the most part to her own devices. As they had arrived in Sanford on Monday, Marjorie's mother had decided to give her daughter an opportunity to accustom herself to her new home and surroundings before allowing her to enter the high school. So the day for Marjorie's initial appearance in "The Sanford High School for Girls" had been set for the following Monday.

It was now Friday afternoon. Marjorie had spent the morning in writing a fifteen-page letter to Mary, the minor refrain of which was: "I can't tell you how much I miss you, Mary," and which contained views regarding her future high school career that were far from being optimistic. She had not finished her letter. She decided to leave it open until after luncheon and, laying it aside for the time, she had tripped down stairs and out doors.

"What are you going to do this afternoon, dear?" asked her mother as Marjorie slipped into place at the luncheon table.

"I don't know, Mother," was the almost doleful reply. "I thought I might take a walk up Orchard street as far as Sargent's, that cunning little confectioner's shop on the corner. Perhaps, if I go, I may see something interesting to tell Mary. I haven't finished my letter."

Marjorie did not add that her walk would include a last stroll past the towering gray walls of a certain stone building on Lincoln avenue, which bore over its massive oak doors the inscription, "The Sanford High School for Girls." Almost every day since her arrival, she had visited it, viewing it speculatively and with a curious kind of apprehension. She was not afraid to plunge into her new school life, but deep down in her heart she felt some little misgiving. What if the new girls proved to be neither likable nor companionable? What if she liked them but they did not like her? She had just begun the same apprehensive train of thought that had been disturbing her peace of mind for the last four days when her mother's voice broke the spell.

"If you are going that far I wish you would go on to Parke & Whitfield's for me. I should like you to match this embroidery silk. I have not enough of it to finish this collar and cuff set I am making for you."

"I'll be your faithful servant and execute all your commissions, mum," declared Marjorie with a little obeisance, her spirits rising a little at the prospect of actual errands to perform. She was already tired of aimlessly wandering along the wide, well-kept streets of Sanford, feeling herself to be quite out of things. Even errands were actual blessings sometimes, she decided, as a little later, she ran upstairs to dress.

"May I wear my best suit and hat, Mother?" she called anxiously down from the head of the stairs. "It's such a lovely day, I'm sure it won't rain, snow, hail or do anything else to spoil them."

"Very well," answered Mrs. Dean, placidly.

With a gurgle of delight Marjorie hurried into her room to put on her new brown suit, which had the mark of a well-known tailor in the coat, and her best hat, on which all the Franklin High girls had set their seal of approval. She had shoes and gloves to match her suit, too, and her dancing brown eyes and fluffy brown hair were the last touches needed to complete the dainty little study in brown.

"Don't I look nice in this suit?" she asked her mother saucily, turning slowly around before the living-room mirror. "Aren't you and father perfect dears to let me have it, though?" She whirled and descended upon her mother with outstretched arms, enveloping her in an ecstatic hug that sadly disturbed the proper angle of her brown velvet hat.

"Don't be gone too long," reminded her mother. "You know father has promised us tickets for the theatre to-night. We shall have an early dinner."

"All right, I'll remember, Captain." With a brisk touching of her hand to her hat brim in salute Marjorie vanished through the door, to reappear a moment later at the living-room window, flash a merry smile at her mother, about face and march down the walk in true military style.

Long before when Marjorie was a tiny girl she had shown an unusual preference for soldiers. She had owned enough wooden soldiers to make a regiment and was never at a loss to invent war games in which they figured. Sometimes, when she tired of her stiff, silent armies, which could only move as she willed, she inveigled her father or mother into being the hero, the enemy, the traitor or whatever her active imagination chose to suggest. Her parents, amused at her boyish love of military things, encouraged her in her play and entered into it with as much spirit as the child herself. Her father, who had once been an officer in the National Guard, taught her the manual of arms and she had learned it with a will.

Marjorie's military enthusiasm had been at its height when she met Mary Raymond, who soon became equally fascinated with the stirring play. In time other interests crowded their lives. The hard-worked armies were laid peacefully on their wooden backs to enjoy a long, undisturbed rest, while Marjorie and Mary became soldiers instead, addressing Mr. Dean as "General," Mrs. Dean as "Captain," and bestowing upon themselves the rank of ordinary enlisted soldiers who must earn their promotion by loyal and faithful service.

Mr. Dean had been rather chary of promotions, frequently reminding his little detachment that it is a far cry from the ranks of a private to that of a commissioned officer. So when their parting came, Mary and Marjorie had just received their commissions as second lieutenants, their awards of faithful service in the grammar school.

Lieutenant Marjorie smiled, then sighed, as she started on her walk. The salute she had just given brought a flood of memories of Mary. She felt she would not mind exploring this strange, new, high school territory if Mary were with her. She was sure no girl in Sanford could understand her as Mary had. On two different afternoons she had stood across the street from the school at the time of dismissal. She had eagerly watched the great oak doors open wide and the long lines of girls file out, waking the still October air with their merry voices. She had been particularly attracted toward one tall, lithe, graceful girl whose golden hair and brown eyes made her unusually lovely. At first sight of her, lonely, imaginative Marjorie had named her "The Picture Girl," and had decided that she was a darling. She had noticed that the pretty girl was always the center of a group and she had also noted that one small, black-haired girl with an elfish face, who wore the most exquisite clothes invariably walked at the tall girl's side. There was a pink-cheeked girl, too, with laughing blue eyes and dimples, and a fair-haired, serious-faced girl, who reminded Marjorie of Alice Duval. They usually formed part of the group about the tall girl and her dark companion, and there was also a very short, stout girl who puffed along anxiously in the rear of the group as though never quite able to catch up.

Marjorie had already imagined much concerning this particular knot of girls, and her desire to see them again before entering school was responsible for her walk down Lincoln avenue that sunny fall afternoon. She would do her errands first, she decided, then, returning by the way of the school, pass there just at the time that the afternoon session was dismissed. She went about her far-from-arduous commissions in leisurely fashion, now and then glancing at her châtelaine watch to make sure of the time. Three o'clock saw the daily procession of girls down the high school steps, and released from classes for the day. She did not intend to miss them.

It was twenty minutes to three when Marjorie finished a remarkable concoction of nuts, chocolate syrup and ice cream, a kind of glorified nut sundae, rejoicing in the name of "Sargent Nectar," and left the smart little confectioner's shop. As she neared the school building her eyes suddenly became riveted upon a slim, blue-clad figure that hesitated for on instant at the top of the high steps then ran lightly down and came hurrying toward where she stood.

"The advance guard," declared Marjorie half aloud. Then, as her eyes sought the approaching girl: "Why, she looks like Mary! And she's been crying! I'm going to speak to her." She took an impulsive step forward as the stranger came abreast of her and began:

"Won't you——"

Marjorie's speech ended abruptly. The weeping girl cast one startled glance toward her from a pair of wet blue eyes, lunged by her without speaking and, breaking into a run, turned the corner and disappeared from view. Marjorie surveyed the back of the rapidly vanishing yellow head with rueful surprise. Then she gave a short laugh.

"I should have known better," she reflected. "Of course, she'd hardly care to tell her personal affairs to the first one who asks her. But she made me think of Mary. Oh, dear, I'm so homesick. Not even my new suit and hat can make me forget that. I wouldn't have mother know it for the world. I believe she is a wee bit homesick, too."

Marjorie paused for an instant at her accustomed place on the opposite side of the street, undecided whether to loiter there and once more watch her future companions pass out of school or to go on about her business. Suddenly the school doors swung wide and the pupils began flocking out. The little stranger yielded to the temptation to linger long enough to watch the five girls pass in whom she had become interested. They were among the last to emerge and, the moment they reached the steps, their voices rose in a confused babble, each one determined to make herself heard above the others.

"I knew she wouldn't do it," shrilled the stout girl, as they neared Marjorie. "She's too stingy for words. That's the third time she's refused to go into things with the rest of us."

"Be still," reminded the Picture Girl; "she might have very good reasons——"

"Good reasons," scornfully mimicked the little dark girl, her black eyes glittering angrily. "It was only because the plan was mine. She hates me, and you all know why. I don't think you ought to stand up for her, Muriel. You know how deceitful she is and what unkind things she said about me."

"I'm not standing up for her," contradicted Muriel, but her tones lacked force. "I only felt a little bit sorry for her. She looked ready to cry all the afternoon. I think she went home early to avoid meeting us."

"That proves she is a coward," was the triumphant retort. "Remember——" With a sudden swift movement she rose on tiptoe and, drawing the Picture Girl's head to the level of her mouth, whispered something to her. The fair-haired girl looked annoyed, the fat girl openly sulky and the dimpled girl disapproving. Exchanging significant glances, they walked on ahead of the other two.

Without the slightest intention of being an eavesdropper, Marjorie had heard every word of the loud-spoken conversation. Her eyes were fixed in fascination upon the dark, sharp-featured face so close to the fair, beautiful one. She suddenly recalled a picture she had once seen called "The Evil Genius," in which a dark, mocking face peered over the shoulder of a young man who sat at a table as though in deep thought. This girl's vivid face bore a slight resemblance to that of the Evil Genius, and it was not until the end of Marjorie's junior year in Sanford that this sinister impression faded and disappeared forever.

When the little company had passed on down the street, Marjorie turned and followed them from a distance. For several blocks her way lay in the same direction, but as she turned into her own street she swept a last glance toward the five girls. She wondered whom they had been discussing so freely. She was vaguely disappointed in the Picture Girl, who seemed to her independent mind too easily influenced by the Evil Genius. Marjorie had already begun to think of the small, dark girl as that. She was glad not to be the girl they had discussed. Then, her thought changing, a vision of two wet blue eyes and a tear-stained face set in fluffy yellow curls came to her, and Marjorie knew that she had seen the object of their discussion. A wave of sympathy for the offender swept over her. "I don't believe she could do anything deceitful or horrid," she reflected stoutly. "Her eyes are as true and as blue as Mary's. I'm going to like her and be her friend, if she'll let me, for she certainly seems to need one. I did so want to be friends with the Picture Girl, but I can't help wishing she had been just a little bit braver."

While Marjorie strolled thoughtfully home, deep in her own cogitations, the five girls, having joined forces again, were discussing her.

"Did you see that pretty girl standing across from the school as we came out?" asked Susan Atwell, the girl with the dimples.

"Yes," returned Irma Linton. "I noticed her there the other day, too. I wonder who she can be."

"I don't know," said Muriel Harding. "She is awfully sweet though, and dresses beautifully. She——"

"I know all about her," interrupted Geraldine Macy. "Her father is the new manager for Preston & Haines. They only moved here from the city last week. Her name is Dean. That is, her last name. I don't know her other name."

"I am surprised that you don't know that," was the sarcastic comment of Mignon La Salle, the little dark girl.

"You needn't be," flung back the stout girl. "There are lots of things I don't know that I'd like to know. For instance——"

"Don't be cross, Jerry," interrupted Mignon, hastily. "I was only teasing you." She cast a peculiar glance at the ruffled Jerry from under her heavy lashes which the young woman failed to catch. "Tell us some more about this new girl. I really didn't pay hardly any attention to her to-day."

"There isn't anything more to tell that I know of," muttered Jerry, sulkily, her desire to distribute news quite gone. "Wait until Monday and see. I know she's going to enter Sanford High and that she's a freshman."

"Then as freshmen it's our solemn duty to be nice to her and make her feel at home," stated Muriel, seriously.

Mignon La Salle shrugged her thin shoulders. "Perhaps," she said, without enthusiasm. "I shall wait until I see her before I decide that."

Meanwhile, Marjorie had reached home, and, seated before the library table, was writing for dear life on the letter she had begun to Mary. So far she had had nothing to tell her chum regarding the young women who were to be her classmates. To be sure, what she had seen and heard that afternoon had amounted to nothing, but the girl who looked like Mary had set her to longing all over again to be able, just for one afternoon, to sit side by side on the front steps with her childhood's friend and talk things over.

"You can't imagine, Mary," she wrote, "how sorry I felt when I saw that poor girl crying with your eyes. They were just like yours. I forgot everything except that she looked like you, and asked her what the trouble was. Of course, she didn't answer me, but actually ran down the street. I should have known better, but I felt so terribly sympathetic. 'Terribly' is the only word that expresses it. Right after she had gone the others began to come out of school, and at last the five girls I told you about came out. They were all talking at once, but I heard the horrid, sharp-faced, dark girl say that someone was stingy and deceitful and a lot of other unpleasant things. I thought the Picture Girl was going to stand up for the person, but that mean little Evil Genius wouldn't let her. Then all at once it came to me that it was this Mary girl they were talking about. It was really this one dark girl who said most of the mean things. The others just listened to her. At any rate, I'm going to find out who the Mary girl is and try to be a friend to her just because she looks like you. Don't imagine I could ever like her better than you, because you know I couldn't. But it's a true soldier's duty to stand by his comrades on the firing line, you know, and I am going to be this girl's freshman comrade, and, if she's one-half as nice as you, I'll be ready to help her fight her battles.

"Monday is the great day. I dread it, and yet I am looking forward to it. I like the outside of the school, but will I like the inside? Mother is going to the principal's office with me. I hope I sha'n't have to try a lot of tiresome examinations. I have forgotten everything I ever knew, and the weather has been too pleasant to study. This is such a pretty town, with plenty of nice walks. If only you were here it would be quite perfect. I do hope you can come and visit me at Easter. Must stop now, as I hear mother calling me. We are going to walk down to meet father. With my dearest love. Write soon.

"Yours always,

"Marjorie."

Marjorie folded, addressed and stamped her letter, then catching her hat from the hallrack ran out the front door to overtake her mother who had walked on ahead.

"I finished my letter to Mary," she held it up for inspection, "and I've something to report, Captain."

"I am ready to hear you," smiled her mother, as they walked on arm in arm.

For the second time Marjorie related her little adventure, ending with her resolve to learn to know and befriend, if necessary, the girl who looked like Mary. Nor did she have the slightest premonition of how much this readily-avowed championing of a stranger was to cost her.

CHAPTER IV

SANFORD'S LATEST FRESHMAN

"Will you tell me the way to the principal's office, please?"

A clear voice broke in upon the conversation of two girls who had paused before the broad stairway leading to the second floor of the Sanford High School for a last word before separating for their morning recitations.

At the sound of the soft, interrupting voice, which contained a touch of perplexity in its tones, both girls turned quickly to regard the owner. They saw an attractive little figure, wearing a dainty blue cloth gown, which was set off by hand-embroidered cuffs and an open rolling collar of sheerest white. From under a smart blue hat escaped a wealth of soft, brown curls, while two brown eyes looked into theirs with an expression of appeal that brought forth instant reply.

"Miss Archer's office is the last room on the east side of the second-floor corridor. I am going there now and shall be glad to show you the way," was the quick response of the taller of the two girls, accompanied by a cheery smile that warmed Marjorie Dean's heart and made her feel the least bit less of a stranger in this strange land which she was about to explore.

"Thank you," she returned gratefully, trying to smile in an equally friendly manner.

Marjorie's first day of school had begun far from propitiously. She had not reckoned on making her initial appearance in Sanford High School alone. It had been planned that her mother should accompany her, but when Monday morning came, her beloved captain had awakened with a racking headache, which meant nothing less than lying in bed for a long, pain-filled day in a darkened room.

Torn between sympathy for her mother and her own disappointment, Marjorie had experienced a desire to go to her captain's room and cry her eyes out, but being fashioned of sturdier stuff, she made a desperate effort to brace up and be a good soldier. This was just another of those miserable "vicissitudes" that no one could foresee. She must face it without grumbling. Her father had already telephoned for a physician when she entered her mother's room, and Marjorie put on her sweetest smile as she kissed her mother and assured her that she didn't in the least mind going to school alone.

As she followed the young woman up the stairs and down the long corridor Marjorie felt her heart beat a little faster. Her low spirits of the early morning began to rise. How good it seemed actually to be in school again! And what a beautiful school it was! Even Franklin would appear dingy beside it. She gazed appreciatively at the high ceiling and the shining oak wainscotings of the wide corridor through which she was passing. When her guide, who was tall, thin and plain of face, opened the last door on the right and ushered her into a beautiful sunshiny office which seemed more like a living-room than a place wherein business was transacted, Marjorie uttered an involuntary, "Oh, how lovely!"

"Yes, isn't it though," returned the tall girl. "This is Miss Archer's own idea, and, so far, it's proving a brilliant success. That is, we all think so. Is Miss Archer in her private office?" she asked the young woman who had risen from her desk near the door and came forward to receive them.

Marjorie would have liked to ask her new acquaintance what she meant, but at that moment a door at the farther end of the room opened and a stately, black-haired woman, with just a suspicion of gray at her temples, emerged. She turned a pair of grave, deep-set eyes upon the tall girl and said, pleasantly: "Well, Ellen, what can I do for you this morning?"

"Oh, Miss Archer!" exclaimed the tall girl, eagerly, with an impulsive step forward, "you haven't forbidden basketball this year, have you? Stella and I couldn't believe our ears when we heard it this morning!" It was evident that the impetuous Ellen was on the best possible terms with her principal.

"I don't remember having issued an order to that effect," smiled Miss Archer. "Where did you hear that bit of news?"

Ellen Seymour's plain face flushed, then paled. "It was just a rumor," she replied with reluctance. "I'd rather not mention names. Still, when I heard it, I could not rest until I had asked you. The sophomores hope to do something wonderful this year. We couldn't bear to believe for a minute that there would be no basketball. We had planned to have a tryout some day this week, after school. I'm so glad," she added fervently. "Thank you, Miss Archer. Oh, pardon me," she turned to Marjorie, "this is Miss Archer, our principal. Miss Archer, this young lady wishes to see you. I met her in the corridor downstairs and volunteered my services as guide."

With a courteous nod to Marjorie, the tall girl left the room and the principal turned her attention toward the prospective freshman.

At the calm, kindly inquiry of the gray eyes Marjorie's feeling of shyness vanished, and she said in her most soldierly manner, as though speaking to her mother: "Miss Archer, my name is Marjorie Dean, and I wish to enter the freshman class of Sanford High School. We moved to Sanford from the city of B——. We have been here just a week. I was a freshman in Franklin High School at B——."

Miss Archer took the young girl's hand in hers. Her rather stern face was lighted with a welcoming smile. Marjorie's direct speech and frank, honest eyes had pleased the older woman.

"I am glad to know that we are to have a new pupil," she said cordially. "The freshman class is smaller than usual this year. So many girls leave school when their grammar school course is finished. I wish we could persuade these mothers and fathers to let their daughters have at least a year of high school. It would help them so much in whatever kind of work they elected to do later."

"That is what mother says," returned Marjorie, quickly. "My mother intended to come with me to-day, but was unable to do so." She did not go into details. Young as she was, Marjorie had a horror of discussing her personal affairs with a stranger. "She will call upon you later."

"I shall be pleased to meet your mother," Miss Archer made courteous answer. "The first and most important matter to be considered this morning is your class standing. Let me see. B—— is in the same state as the town of Sanford. I believe the system of credits is the same in all the high schools throughout this state, as the examinations come from the state board at the capital. What studies had you begun at B——?"

"English composition, algebra, physiology, American history and French," recited Marjorie, dutifully.

Miss Archer raised her eyebrows. "You are ambitious. We usually allow our pupils to carry only four subjects."

"But these are quite easy subjects," pleaded Marjorie; "that is, all except algebra. I am not especially clever in mathematics. I am obliged to study very hard to make good recitations. Still, I should like to continue with the subjects I have begun. Won't you try me until the end of the first term?" she added, a coaxing note in her voice.

"I will at least try you for a week or two. Then if I find that you are not overtaxing your strength you may go on with them."

"Thank you." Marjorie's relieved tone caused the principal to smile again. It was not usual for a pupil to show concern over the prospect of losing a subject. Many of the students rebelled at having to carry four subjects.

"Have you your grammar school certificate with you?" asked Miss Archer, the smile giving way to a businesslike expression.

Marjorie handed the principal the large envelope she had been carrying. Miss Archer drew forth a square of thick white paper, ornamented with the red seal by which the state board of school commissioners had signified their approval of Marjorie Dean and her work in the grammar school.

The older woman read it carefully. "Yes, this is, as I thought the same form of certificate. From this moment on you are a freshman in Sanford High School, Miss Dean. I trust that you will be happy here. Sanford has the reputation of being one of the finest schools in the state. I am going to assign you to a seat in the study hall at once. Miss Merton is in charge there. She will give you a printed form of our curriculum of study. School opens at nine o'clock in the morning. The morning session lasts until twelve o'clock. We have an hour and a quarter for luncheon, and our last recitation for the day is over at half past three o'clock. We have devotional exercises in the chapel on Monday and Friday mornings, and the course in gymnastics is optional. There are, of course, many other things regarding the regulations of the school which you will gradually come to know."

"Miss Arnold," the thin-faced, sharp-eyed young woman, who had been covertly appraising Marjorie during her talk with Miss Archer, came languidly forward. "This is Miss Dean." The two girls bowed rather distantly. Marjorie had conceived an instant and violent dislike for this lynx-eyed stranger. "Take Miss Dean to the locker room, then to Miss Merton. Say to Miss Merton that Miss Dean is a freshman, and that I wish her assigned to a desk in the freshman section."

With a last glance of pleasant approval, which Marjorie's pretty face, dainty attire and frank, yet modest bearing had evoked, the principal retired to her inner office, and Marjorie obediently followed her guide, who, without speaking, set off down the corridor at almost unnecessary speed. "This way," she directed curtly as they reached the main corridor. They passed down the corridor, descended a second stairway and brought up directly in front of long rows of lockers. Within five minutes Marjorie's hat had been put away, and she had received a locker key. This done, her companion hurried her upstairs and down the wide corridor through which they had first come.

Then she suddenly opened a door, and Marjorie found herself in an enormous square room, which contained row upon row of shining oak desks, occupied by what seemed to her hundreds of pupils. In reality there were not more than two hundred and forty persons in the room, but in the eyes of the little stranger everything was quadrupled. How different it was from Franklin! So this was the study hall, one of the things on which the school prided itself. In front of the rows of desks was one large desk on a small raised platform, reminding Marjorie of an island in the midst of a sea. At the desk sat a small, gray-haired woman, who peered suspiciously over her glasses at Marjorie as she was lifelessly introduced by Miss Arnold.

"I don't like her at all," was the young girl's inward comment as she walked behind the stiff, uncompromising, black-clothed back to a desk almost in the middle of the last row of seats on the east side. But Marjorie experienced a little shiver of delight as she seated herself, for directly in front of her, and gazing at her with reassuring, smiling eyes, was the Picture Girl.

CHAPTER V

GETTING ACQUAINTED WITH THE PICTURE GIRL

"Welcome to Sanford," whispered the girl, "and to the freshman class. I was sure when I saw you the other day you couldn't be anything other than a freshman."

Marjorie flushed, then smiled faintly. "I didn't think any of the girls would remember me," she confessed.

"Oh, I remember you perfectly. You were across the street from school on three different days, weren't you?"

Marjorie nodded. "I just had to come down and get acquainted with the outside of the school. I was awfully curious about it."

"Miss Harding," a cold voice at their elbows caused both girls to start. So intent had they been on their conversation that they had not noticed Miss Merton's approach, "you may answer any questions Miss Dean wishes to ask regarding our course of study here as set forth in our curriculum." She laid a closely printed sheet of paper before Marjorie. "This does not mean, however, the personal conversation in which, I am sorry to say, you appeared to be engrossed when I approached. Remember, Miss Dean, that personal conversation will neither be excused nor tolerated in the study hall. I trust I shall not have to remind you of this again."

Marjorie watched with unseeing eyes the angular form of the teacher as she retreated to her platform. If Miss Merton had dealt her a blow on her upturned face, it could have hurt no more severely than had this unlooked-for reprimand. She was filled with a choking sense of shame that threatened to end in a burst of angry sobs. The deep blush that had risen to her face receded, leaving her very white. Those students sitting in her immediate vicinity had, of course, heard Miss Merton. She glanced quickly about to encounter two pairs of eyes. One pair was blue and, it seemed to the embarrassed newcomer, sympathetic. Their owner was the "Mary" girl, who sat two seats behind her in the next aisle. The other pair was cruelly mocking, and they belonged to the girl that Marjorie had mentally styled the Evil Genius. Something in their taunting depths stirred an hitherto unawakened chord in gentle Marjorie Dean. She returned the insolent gaze with one so full of steady strength and defiance that the girl's eyes dropped before it and she devoted herself assiduously to the open book which she held in her hand.

"Don't mind Miss Merton," whispered Muriel, comfortingly. "She is the worst crank I ever saw. No one likes her. I don't believe even Miss Archer does. She's been here for ages, so the Board of Education thinks that Sanford High can't run without her, I guess."

"I'm so mortified and ashamed," murmured Marjorie. "On my first day, too."

"Don't think about it," soothed Muriel. "What studies are you going to take? I hope you will recite in some of my classes. Wait a moment. I'll come back there and sit with you; then we'll make less noise. Miss Merton told me to help you, you know," she reminded, with a soft chuckle.

The fair head and the dark one bent earnestly over the printed sheet. Marjorie whispered her list of subjects to her new friend, who jotted them down on the margin of the program.

"How about . English Comp?" she asked. "That's my section."

Marjorie nodded her approval.

"Then you can recite algebra with me at ., and there's a first-year French class at .. That brings three subjects in the morning. Now, let me see about your history. If you can make your history and physiology come the first two periods in the afternoon, you will be through by three o'clock and can have that last half hour for study or gym, or whatever you like. I am carrying only four subjects, so I have nothing but physical geography in the afternoon. I am through reciting every day by o'clock, so I learn most of my lessons in school and hardly ever take my books home. If I were you, I'd drop one subject—American History, for instance. You can study it later. The freshman class is planning a lot of good times for this winter, and, of course, you want to be in them, too, don't you?"

"I should say so," beamed Marjorie. "Still," her face sobering, "I think I won't drop history. It's easy, and I love it."

"Well, I don't," emphasized Muriel. "By the way, do you play basketball?"

"I played left guard on our team last year, and I had just been chosen for center on the freshman team, at Franklin High, when I left there," was the whispered reply.

"That's encouraging," declared Muriel. "We haven't chosen our team yet. We are to have a tryout at four o'clock on Friday afternoon in the gymnasium. You can go to the meeting with me, although you will have met most of the freshman class before Friday. Oh, yes, did Miss Archer tell you that we report in the study hall at half-past eight o'clock on Monday and Friday mornings? We have chapel exercises, and woe be unto you if you are late. It's an unforgivable offense in Miss Merton's eyes to walk into chapel after the service has begun. If you are late, you take particular pains to linger around the corridor until the line comes out of chapel, then you slide into your section and march into the study hall as boldly as though you'd never been late in your life," ended Muriel with a giggle, which she promptly smothered.

"But what if Miss Merton sees one?"

Muriel made a little resigned gesture. "Try it some day and see. There's the .bell. Come along. If we hurry we'll have a minute with the girls before class begins. All of my chums recite English this first hour. You needn't stop at Miss Merton's desk. It'll be all right."

Marjorie walked down the aisle behind Muriel, looking rather worried. Then she touched Muriel's arm. "I think I'd rather stop and speak to Miss Merton," she said with soft decision.

"All right," the response came indifferently as Muriel, a bored look on her youthful face, walked on ahead.

Marjorie walked bravely up to the teacher. "Miss Merton, I have arranged my studies and recitation hours. Miss Harding is going to show me the way to the English composition class."

Miss Merton stared coldly at the girl's vivid, colorless face, framed in its soft brown curls. Her own youth had been prim and narrow, and she felt that she almost hated this girl whose expressive features gave promise of remarkable personality and abundant joy of living.

"Very well." The disagreeable note of dismissal in the teacher's voice angered Marjorie.

"I'll never again speak to her unless it's positively necessary," she resolved resentfully. "I wish I'd taken Miss Harding's advice."

"Well, did she snap your head off?" inquired Muriel as Marjorie joined her.

"No," was the brief answer.

"It's a wonder. There goes the third bell. It's on to English comp for us. I won't have time to introduce you to the girls. We'll have to wait until noon. Miss Flint teaches English. She's a dear, and everyone likes her."

Muriel's voice dropped on her last speech, for they were now entering the classroom. At the first flat-topped desk in one corner of the room sat a small, fair woman with a sweet, sunshiny face that quite won Marjorie to her.

"Miss Flint, this is Miss Dean," began Muriel, as they stopped before the desk. "She is a freshman and has just been registered in the study hall by Miss Merton."

A long, earnest glance passed between teacher and pupil, then Marjorie felt her hand taken between two small, warm palms. "I am sure Miss Dean and I are going to be friends," said a sweet, reassuring voice that amply made up for Miss Merton's stiffness. "Are you a stranger in Sanford, my dear? I am sure I have never seen you before."

"We have lived here a week," smiled Marjorie. "We moved here from B——."

"How interesting. Were you a student of Franklin High School? I have a dear friend who teaches English there."

"Oh!" exclaimed Marjorie, her eyes sparkling, "do you mean Miss Fielding?"

"Yes," returned Miss Flint. "We were best friends during our college days, too. Hampton College is our alma mater."

"That is where I hope to go when I finish high school. Miss Fielding has told me so many nice things about Hampton," was Marjorie's eager reply. Then she added impetuously, "I'm going to like Sanford, too. I'm quite sure of it."

"That is the right spirit in which to begin your work here," was the instant response. "I will assign you to that last seat in the third row. We do not change seats. Each girl is given her own place for the year."

Marjorie thanked Miss Flint, and made her way to the seat indicated. The sound of footsteps in the corridor had ceased. A tall girl in the front row of desks slipped from her seat and closed the door. Miss Flint rose, faced her class, and the recitation began.

After the class was dismissed Miss Flint detained Marjorie for a moment to ask a few questions regarding her text and note books. Muriel waited in the corridor. Her face wore an expression of extreme satisfaction. It looked as though the new freshman might be a distinct addition to the critical little company of girls who had set themselves as rulers and arbiters of the freshman class. She was pretty, wore lovely clothes, lived in a big house in a select neighborhood, had played center on a city basketball team, and was the friend of Miss Flint's friend. To be sure, Mignon La Salle might raise some objection to the newcomer. Mignon was so unreasonably jealous. But for all her money, Mignon must not be allowed always to have her own way. Muriel was sure the rest of the girls would be quite in favor of adding Marjorie Dean to their number. They needed one more girl to complete their sextette. To Marjorie should fall the honor.

"I'll introduce her to the girls this noon, and let them look her over. Then I'll have a talk with them to-night and see what they think," planned Muriel as she went back to the study hall at Marjorie's side.

There was a hurried exchange of books, then Marjorie was rushed off to her algebra recitation. Here she found herself at least two weeks ahead of the others, and was able to solve a problem at the blackboard that had puzzled several members of the class, thereby winning a reputation for herself as a mathematician to which it afterward proved anything but easy to live up to.

While in both her English and algebra classes Marjorie had searched the room with alert eyes for the girl who looked like Mary. She felt vaguely disappointed. She had hoped to come into closer contact with her. She liked Muriel, she decided, but she did not altogether understand her half-cordial, half-joking manner. She was rather glad that she was to go to her French class alone. She had told Muriel not to bother. She could find the classroom by herself.

As she clicked down the short, left-hand, third floor corridor, she saw just ahead of her a little blue-clad figure passing through the very doorway for which she was making. An instant and she too had entered the room. She stared about her, then walked to a seat directly opposite to the one now occupied by the girl that looked like Mary. For a brief moment the girl eyed Marjorie indifferently, then something in the scrutiny of the other girl evidently annoyed her. She drew her straight dark brows together in a displeased frown, and deliberately turned her face away.

By this time perhaps a dozen girls had entered, and, as the clang of the third bell echoed through the school, an alert little man with a thin, sensitive face and timid brown eyes, bustled into the room and carefully closed the door. Hardly had he taken his hand from the knob when the door was flung open, this time to admit a sharp-featured girl with bright, dark eyes and a cruel, thin-lipped mouth. Smiling maliciously, she swung the door shut with an echoing bang. The meek little professor looked reproachfully at the offender, who did not even appear to see him.

"The Evil Genius," recognized Marjorie. Her eyes strayed furtively toward the Mary girl, who had not paid the slightest attention to this late arrival. "What a hateful person that black-eyed girl is," ran on Marjorie's thoughts. "I know it was she who made that nice girl cry the other day. I wish she wasn't quite so distant. The nice girl, I mean. Oh, dear. I forgot to go up to the professor's desk and register. That's his fault. He came in late. He'll see me in a minute and ask who I am."

To her extreme surprise, the little man paid no particular attention to her, but, opening his grammar, began the giving out of the next day's lesson. This he explained volubly and with many gestures. Marjorie's lips curved into a half smile as she compared this rather noisy instructor with Professor Rousseau, of Franklin. Later, when he called upon his pupils to recite, however, he was a different being. His politely sarcastic arraignment of those who floundered through the lessons, accompanied by certain ominous marks he placed after their names in a fat black book that lay on his desk, plainly showed that, despite his mild appearance, he was a force yet to be reckoned with.

"I hope he doesn't notice me until class is over," fidgeted Marjorie. "It surely must be time for that bell to ring." She began nervously to count those who were due to recite before her turn came. It would be so embarrassing to do her explaining before this group of strange girls, particularly before the Evil Genius. Ah, she had begun to read! And how beautifully she read French! The critical professor was listening to the smooth flow of words that tripped from her tongue with approbation written on every feature. "She must have studied French before," speculated Marjorie, as the professor directed the next girl to go on with the exercise; "or else she is French. I believe she is. Oh, dear, only two more girls."

Clang! sounded the bell.

"Thank goodness," breathed the relieved freshman.

There was a general closing of books. "To-morrow I shall geev you a wreetten test," warned Professor Fontaine. Then the second bell rang, and the class filed out of the room.

"Eet ees not strange that I haf overlooked you, Mademoiselle," explained Professor Fontaine five minutes later, after listening to Marjorie's apology for not presenting herself to him before class. "The freshmen like to make so many alterations in their programs. They haf soch good excuses for changeeng classes, but, sometimes, too, they do not tell me. Eet maks exasperation." He waved his hands comprehensively. "I am pleased," he added, with true French courtesy, "to haf another pupil. Ees eet that you like the French, Mademoiselle Dean?"

"It is a beautiful language, Professor Fontaine," Marjorie assured him. "I have only begun learning it, but I like it so much."

"C'est vrai," murmured the delighted professor. "La Francais est une belle langue. If, then, you like it, you weel study your lessons, n'est pas?"

"I'll try very hard to make good recitations. I will bring my books to-morrow. We used the same grammar at Franklin High School."

Marjorie hastened back to the study hall to find it empty. The clock on the north wall pointed significant hands to ten minutes past twelve. The Picture Girl had said that she wished Marjorie to meet her friends, but she was not waiting. It was disappointing, but her own fault, thought the lonely freshman as she left the study hall and went slowly downstairs to the locker room. She gave an impatient sigh as she pinned on her hat. Exploring new territory wasn't half so interesting as she could wish. Then a light footstep sounded at her side. A dignified little voice said, stiffly, "Will you please allow me to get my hat?"

Marjorie whirled about in amazement. Could she believe her eyes? The voice belonged to the Mary girl; they were to share the same locker.

CHAPTER VI

THE PLEDGE

"Oh, I am so glad we are to have a locker together!" exclaimed Marjorie, impulsively. "I've been very anxious to know you. I really owe you an apology. I spoke to you in the street the other day. I don't know what you thought of me, but you look so much like my dearest chum in B—— that I called to you before I realized what I was doing."

The other girl regarded Marjorie with the suspicious, uneasy eyes of a cornered animal. Then, without answering, she reached for her hat and was about to go silently on her way, when something in Marjorie's gracious words seemed to touch her and she said, grudgingly, "I remember you."

"That's nice," beamed Marjorie. "I was afraid you wouldn't. Let me tell you about my chum." She launched forth in an enthusiastic description of Mary Raymond and of their long friendship. "I wrote Mary about having seen a girl that looked like her. She will be very curious to see you. She's coming to visit me some time during the year. So I hope you and I will be friends. But I haven't even told you who I am. My name is Marjorie Dean. Won't you please tell me yours?" She offered her hand winningly, but the strange, self-contained young girl ignored it.

"My name is Constance Stevens." Her voice was coldly reluctant, carrying with it an unmistakable rebuff.

Marjorie drew back, puzzled and hurt. She was not used to having her friendly overtures rejected. The blue-eyed girl saw the shrinking movement, and, stirred by some hitherto unknown impulse, stretched forth her hand. "Please forgive me for being so rude," she said contritely. "It is awfully sweet in you to tell me about your chum and to say that you wish to be my friend. You are the first girl, who has been so nice with me since I came to Sanford. How I hate them!" Her expressive face darkened and her blue eyes became filled with brooding, sullen anger.

"Are you going home to luncheon now?" asked Marjorie, with a view toward keeping away from disagreeable subjects.

The other girl nodded, then, pinning on her hat, the two left the building. Marjorie wished to ask questions, but she did not know how to begin with this strange, moody girl. There were so many things to say. "Do you play basketball?" she asked, almost timidly, when they had traversed three blocks in silence.

Constance shook her head. "I don't even know the game, let alone trying to play it. Do you play?"

"Yes. I have played every position on the team. I was chosen for center of the freshman team at Franklin High just before I came here. One of the freshmen has asked me to go to the tryout on Friday."

The Mary girl looked wistfully at Marjorie. "I'm going to tell you something," she announced with finality. "Truly, it's for your own good. You mustn't try to be friends with me. If you do, you'll be sorry. We, my father and I, are nobodies in this town. Father's a broken-down musician who teaches the violin for a living. I've a little lame brother, and we take care of a poor old musician, who, people say, is crazy. He isn't, though. He's merely childish.

"People call us Bohemians and gypsies and even vagabonds. They don't understand that our greatest crime is just being poor. The girls in the freshman class make fun of me and call me a tramp and a beggar behind my back. One girl did try to be the least bit pleasant with me, but she soon stopped. We've been in Sanford only two months, but it seems like a hundred years. At first I was glad to think I was going to high school. How I hate it now! But they sha'n't drive me away. I'll get my education in spite of everything." Her lips drew together with resolute purpose.

"So, you see," her voice grew gentle, "you mustn't waste your time upon me. The girls won't like you if you do, and you don't know how dreadful it is to be left out of everything. Of course, you can speak to me, but——" She paused and looked eloquent meaning at Marjorie. Her late aloofness had quite vanished. Her small face was now soft and friendly, making the resemblance to happy-go-lucky Mary Raymond more apparent.

Marjorie laughed. Those who knew her best would have understood that her laughter meant defiance. "I don't choose my friends because they are rich or because others like them. I choose them because I want them myself," she declared with a proud lift of her head. "I knew that someone had been horrid to you the first day I ever saw you. I heard several girls talking of you afterward. At least, I think they were talking of you. I said to myself then that they had misjudged you. So I went home and wrote my letter to Mary. I told mother all about you, too, and that I was going to be your friend, if you would let me. I want you to come and see me and meet mother and father. As for the girls in the freshman class, I'd like to be friends with them, too, but I couldn't do anything so contemptible and unfair as to dislike a girl just because they thought they did. Now, you know what I think about it. Are we going to share our locker and our troubles and our pleasures?"

The tears flashed across Constance Stevens' eyes. Her hand slid into Marjorie's, and thus began a friendship between the two freshmen that was to defy time and change.

They separated on the next corner and, throwing dignity to the winds, Marjorie raced up the long walk and into the house to see if her captain was better.

"I came to report, Captain," she said gently as she tiptoed up to her mother's bed. "How are you, dear?"

"Better, Lieutenant," returned her mother, kissing the pretty, flushed face. "Now for the report."

"You are sure I won't make your head ache with my chatter?"

"No, dear; it is ever so much better now."

Marjorie went faithfully through with the events of the morning. "I had to stand by my colors, Captain. I wouldn't be fit to be a soldier if I didn't know how to stand fast. Just as though it makes any difference whether a girl is rich or poor if she's a dear and one likes her. How can some girls be so silly? They wouldn't be if they had Mary's and my military training. When in doubt ask your captain."

She laughed gaily, then her merry glance changed to one of dismay. "Good gracious! It's fifteen minutes to one. I'll have to eat my luncheon in a hurry." With a hasty kiss Marjorie flitted from the room and down the stairs to the dining-room.

After luncheon she lingered for a brief moment with her mother, then set off for the afternoon session of school. But she could not help wondering as she walked just how it would seem to be in the freshman class but not of it.

The afternoon session of school passed uneventfully for Marjorie. She had returned too late from luncheon to hold more than a few words of conversation with the Picture Girl. In spite of the watchful espionage of Miss Merton, whose eyes seemed riveted to her side of the room, Muriel managed to convey to Marjorie the news that the girls were dying to meet her and were so sorry they had missed her at noon.

"We waited for you more than ten minutes," Muriel whispered guardedly. "Mignon saw you stop at Professor Fontaine's desk. We knew what that meant. It always takes him forever to explain anything. Do you remember a black-haired, black-eyed girl in the French class this morning? She wore the sweetest brown crêpe-de-chine dress. Well, that's Mignon La Salle. Her father is the richest man in Sanford. Mignon could go away to school if she liked, but she doesn't care about it. Tell you more later."

Muriel faced front with a sudden jerk that could mean but one thing. Marjorie cast a fleeting glance at Miss Merton. The teacher was frowning angrily, as though about to deliver a rebuke. Luckily for the two girls, the first recitation bell rang and they stood not upon the order of their going, but went with alacrity. Once outside the study-hall door they were safe.

"I don't know what ails Miss Merton," complained Muriel. "She has never said a word to me before. That's twice to-day she has shown her claws."

"She doesn't like me," said Marjorie, calmly, "and I don't like her. I think she is the rudest teacher I ever knew. It was I, not you that she meant that scolding for this morning."

"Nonsense!" scoffed Muriel. "She likes you as well as she likes the rest of us. I don't believe she is awfully, terribly, fearfully fond of girls. When she was young she must have been one of those stiff, prim goody-goodies; the distressingly snippy sort that made all her friends so tired." Muriel laughed softly.

Marjorie smiled at Muriel's unflattering description of Miss Merton's youth, then her face sobered. In her heart she knew that Miss Merton disliked her, and the knowledge was not pleasant. She made an earnest resolve to overcome the teacher's prejudice. She would make Miss Merton like her.

Muriel went with her as far as the door of the history room, which was in charge of Miss Atkins, a stout, middle-aged woman, who beamed amiably upon Marjorie, entered her name in the class register, motioned her to a front seat and promptly appeared to forget her existence. But though Miss Atkins exhibited small personal interest in her new pupil, such was not the case with regard to the subject which she taught. The lesson dealt with the coming of the Virginia colonists, their settlement in Jamestown and the final burning of the town. Miss Atkins' vivid description of the colonists' determined struggles to gain a foothold in the New World was well worth listening to. The reading of extracts from special reference books pertaining to that gallant expedition into the treacherous forests of an unknown, untried country made the lesson seem doubly interesting. When the recitation was over Marjorie went back to the study hall congratulating herself on the fact that she had not dropped history, and reflecting that no one would ever have suspected Miss Atkins of being so fascinating.

As she groped in her desk for her textbook on physiology, she looked about her for some sign of Constance Stevens. She recollected that she had not seen her in her seat when the afternoon session began. The moment her recitation in physiology was over she hastened to the locker room. No, her new friend's hat was not there. She had not returned to school after luncheon. Marjorie reached for her own hat, vaguely wondering what had happened to keep Constance away from school.

She stood meditatively poking her hatpins in and out of her hat, when the sound of footsteps on the stairs came to her ears. School was over for the day. She put on her hat in a hurry, took a swift peep at herself as she passed the one large mirror that hung at the end of the freshmen's lockers, and ran up the stairs. She would not disappoint Muriel's friends again.

This time she was first on the scene, standing on the identical spot where she had stood the day Constance rushed weeping past her. Why didn't her class come out? Surely she had heard their footsteps on the stairs. But it was fully five minutes before the stream of girls began to issue from the big doors. Then Muriel appeared, surrounded by her friends, and in another instant the girl with the dimples, the fair-haired girl, the stout girl and the Evil Genius were, with varying degrees of friendliness, telling Marjorie Dean that they were glad to meet her.

Susan Atwell said so frankly with a delightful show of dimples. Irma Linton looked the acme of gentle friendliness. Geraldine Macy's face wore an expression of open admiration. Mignon La Salle's greeting, however, was distinctly reserved. To be sure, she smiled; but Muriel, who had been furtively watching her, knew that the French girl was not pleased with the idea of admitting another girl to their fellowship.

"The rest of the girls like her," thought Muriel. "Mignon will find she'll have to give in this time." Purposely, to make sure she was right, she said boldly: "Miss Dean, will you go to the basketball tryout with us on Friday afternoon?"

"Yes, do," urged Geraldine Macy, eagerly.

"We'd love to have you," came from Susan Atwell. "We understand that you are a star player."

"Of course you must," smiled Irma Linton.

The French girl alone hesitated. Her eyes roved speculatively from one face to another, then she said suavely, "Come by all means, Miss Dean. It will be quite interesting."

"Thank you. I shall be pleased to go with you." Marjorie ignored Mignon's slight hesitation, although she had noted it. "I wonder if you are all as fond of basketball as I," she went on quickly. "It's a splendid game, isn't it?"

Her new acquaintances answered with emphasis that it was certainly a great game, and, the ice now broken, they began to ply their new acquaintance with questions. How did she like Sanford? Did it seem strange to her after a big city high school? What subjects had she selected? Had she met any other girls besides themselves?

Marjorie answered them readily enough. She was glad to be one of a crowd of girls again.

"Have you met any other girls?" asked Geraldine Macy, abruptly.

"I met a Miss Seymour before I had even gone as far as Miss Archer's office. She is a delightful girl, isn't she?"

No one of the five girls made answer. The little freshman regarded them perplexedly.

"Mm!" ejaculated Muriel Harding. "You wouldn't think her quite so nice if you knew as much about her as we do. Wait until you see her play basketball. She plays center on the sophomore team, and she makes some very peculiar plays. She's always creating trouble, too. She and some of her sophomore friends seem to have a particular grudge against Mignon. They are forever criticising her playing. They have even gone so far as to say that we don't play fairly; that we are tricky. The idea!" Muriel looked highly offended at the mere idea of any such thing.

Marjorie listened without comment. Muriel's ready tirade against the pleasant-faced sophomore who had willingly offered her services that morning made her feel decidedly uncomfortable. Then Miss Seymour's straightforward speech to Miss Archer came back to her. The sophomore had been generous to her enemies, if they were enemies, in that she had refused to mention any names. Marjorie wondered if Muriel or Mignon would be equally generous in the same circumstances. She resolved to say nothing of what she had been privileged to hear. It was not hers to tell.

Suddenly she divined, rather than saw, Mignon's elfish eyes fixed upon her. "You met another girl, at noon, did you not, Miss Dean?" asked the French girl, with an almost sarcastic inflection.

"Yes; Miss Stevens," was the composed answer. "We share the same locker. She is a nice girl, too, and I like her very much, so, please, don't say anything against her," she ended, in half-smiling warning.

Mignon La Salle's face grew dark. She recognized the challenging note in the new girl's tone. Muriel, too, frowned. Susan Atwell sidled up to Mignon, Irma Linton looked distressed and Geraldine Macy calmly curious as to what would come next. It came in the way of a small tempest, for the French girl lost her temper over Marjorie's retort.

She stamped her foot in childish rage, saying vehemently: "She is a nobody, that Stevens person, and her family are vagabonds. You will make a great mistake if you choose her for your friend." Then, her rage receding as suddenly as it had come, she shrugged her shoulders deprecatingly. "Pardonnez moi." She bowed to Marjorie. "I spoke too strongly. It is not for me to choose Miss Dean's friends." Slipping her arm through Muriel's, she drew her ahead of the others. Susan Atwell took a hurried step forward and caught her other arm, leaving Marjorie to walk between Irma and Geraldine.

"Don't mind her," said Jerry, in a low voice. "She has it in for that Miss Stevens. She, the Stevens girl, did something, no one knows what, to make Mignon angry with her. Mignon says Miss Stevens talked about her and Muriel and Susan believed it, but Irma and I are not so silly."

Two blocks further on Marjorie bade good-bye to the five girls. She said it without enthusiasm. Their carping, quarrelsome attitude had taken all the pleasure from knowing them. She made mental exception in favor of Irma and Jerry. The gentleness of the one and the sturdy, outspoken manner of the other had impressed her favorably. But she was sorely disappointed in Muriel.

Should she tell her mother of the disagreeable ending of her first day? She decided not to do so. She would carry nothing save pleasant tales to her captain to-day. And so that night, when she entered the living-room and found her mother, in a becoming negligee, occupying the wide leather couch by the window, she saluted, like a dutiful soldier, and included in her report only the pleasant happenings of her first, never-to-be-forgotten day in Sanford High School.

CHAPTER VIII

STANDING BY HER COLORS

When Marjorie took her seat in the study hall the next morning, Muriel's greeting was as affable as it had been before the disagreement of the previous afternoon. She even went so far as to whisper, "Don't take Mignon too seriously. She is really dreadfully hurt over the unkind things Miss Stevens has said of her."

Marjorie listened in polite silence to the Picture Girl's rather lame apology in behalf of her friend. She could think of nothing to say. Muriel had turned about in her seat, her eyes fixed expectantly upon the other girl. But just then came an unexpected interruption.

"Miss Dean," shrilled Miss Merton's high, querulous voice, "who gave you permission to leave school before the regular hour of dismissal yesterday afternoon?"

"I did not——" began the astonished girl.

"Young woman, do you mean to contradict me?" thundered Miss Merton.

Marjorie had now risen to her feet. Her pretty face had turned very white, her brown eyes gleamed like two angry flames. "I had no intention of contradicting you, Miss Merton." Her low, steady tones were full of repressed indignation. "What I had begun to say was that I did not know I was expected to return to the study hall after my last class. In the high school which I attended in B—— we went from our last class to our locker rooms. It is, of course, my fault. I should have inquired about it beforehand." The freshman quietly resumed her seat.

Every pair of eyes in the room was turned upon Marjorie.

Miss Merton, however, had no intention of letting her off so easily. "The rules and regulations of another high school do not, in the least, interest me, Miss Dean," she said, with biting sarcasm. "It is my business to see that the rules of Sanford High School are enforced, and I propose to do it. You have been a pupil in this school for only one day, yet I have been obliged to reprimand you on two different occasions. If you annoy me further I shall consider myself fully justified in sending you to Miss Archer."

The ringing of the first recitation bell put an end to the little scene. Marjorie rose from her seat and marched from the study hall, her head held high. If Miss Merton expected her to break down and cry she would find herself sadly mistaken. Muriel overtook her in the corridor. "My, but Miss Merton hates you!" she commented cheerfully, as though enjoying her classmate's discomfiture.

Marjorie made no reply. Her proud spirit was too deeply crushed for words. She went through her recitation in English that morning like one in a dream. Several times during her French hour she gazed appealingly at Constance, but the Mary girl kept her fair head turned resolutely away. She did not appear at her locker either at noon or after school was over, although Marjorie lingered, in the hope that she would come.

So successfully did she manage to steer clear of Marjorie, who was too proud to make advances in the face of Constance's marked avoidance, that, when Friday came and the afternoon session was over, Marjorie was escorted to the gymnasium by the Picture Girl and her friends, who, even to Mignon, believed that the newcomer had been wise and taken their brusque advice.

At least half of the freshman class had elected to try for a place on the team. Miss Randall, the instructor in gymnastics, and several seniors had been chosen to pick the team, and when the six girls arrived on the scene the testing had begun. Mignon La Salle was the first of their group to play. Her almost marvelous agility, her quick, catlike springs and her fleetness of foot called forth unstinted praise from Marjorie. Muriel, too, played a skilful game; so did Susan Atwell. When Marjorie was called upon to play left guard on a team composed of the last lot of aspirants for basketball honors, she advanced to her position rather nervously. Muriel, Mignon, Susan Atwell and two freshmen, whom she did not know, were to oppose her. She wondered if she could play fast enough to keep up with her clever opponents. Then, as she caught the French girl's elfish eyes fixed upon her, mocking incredulity in their depths, she rallied her doubting spirit and resolved to outplay even Mignon.

Fifteen minutes later Marjorie Dean had been chosen to play left guard on a team of which Mignon was center, Muriel, right guard, Susan Atwell, right forward, and a freshman named Harriet Delaney, left forward. Muriel had also been made captain, and several girls were chosen as substitutes.

"Hurrah for the new team!" cried Muriel Harding. "Let's call ourselves the Invincibles. You certainly can play basketball, Miss Dean. How lucky in you to come to Sanford just when we need you. By the way, 'Miss Dean' is too formal. Please let us call you Marjorie. You can call us by our first names. What's the use of so much formality among team-mates?"

Being merely a very human young girl, Marjorie could not help feeling a little bit pleased with herself. She was glad she had played so well. She felt that she had really begun to like her new associates very much. Even Mignon must have her good points; and how wonderfully well she played basketball! Perhaps Constance Stevens had been just a little bit at fault. Certainly she had acted very queerly after that first day when they had pledged their friendship. Had she, Marjorie, been wise to avow unswerving loyalty to a stranger, and all because she looked like Mary Raymond? Marjorie's disquieting reflections were interrupted by something the French girl was saying.

"It was too funny for anything, wasn't it, Muriel?" Mignon laughed with gleeful malice.

"Yes," nodded Muriel. "We gave the sophomores a bad scare."

"What did you do?" asked Irma Linton, curiously.

Seeing that she had the attention of her audience, the French girl began.

"You remember the practice game we played against the sophomores last week? According to my way of thinking, the sophomores played a very rough game. I complained to Miss Seymour, their captain. She laughed at me," Mignon scowled at the remembrance, "so I decided to teach her a lesson."

"I told Muriel about it, and between us we made up a dialogue. It was all about the sophomores' unfair playing, and how surprised they would be when they found themselves forbidden to play basketball. Then we managed to walk out of school behind two girls that always tell everything they know, and recited our dialogue. The next morning Muriel saw one of the girls talking to Miss Seymour for all she was worth, so we know that she faithfully repeated everything she heard. Miss Seymour wouldn't dare go to Miss Archer with it for fear Miss Archer would ask too many questions. You know Miss Archer said last year when Inez Chester made such a fuss about her sprained wrist that if ever again one team reported another for rough playing she would disband the accused team and have Miss Randall select a new one. So I imagine we gave our friends the sophs something to think about."

"But who told you the sophomores would be forbidden to play?" demanded candid Jerry.

"No one told us, silly," retorted Muriel, her color rising. "We simply said they would be surprised when they found themselves forbidden to play. 'When' may mean next week or next month, or next year or century, or any other time. We were only talking for their general edification."

"Then nobody actually said a word about it?" persisted Jerry. "You just made up all that stuff?"

"It didn't do any hurt," began Muriel. "We thought——"

"Don't be such a prig, Jerry," put in Mignon, impatiently. "It isn't half so wicked to play a joke on those stupid sophomores as it is to ask one's mother for money for a fountain pen, and then use the money for candy and ice cream."

There was a chorus of giggles from the girls, in which Jerry did not join. She was eyeing Mignon steadily. "See here, Mignon," she said with offended dignity. "I just want you to know that I told my mother about that money that very same night. I may have my faults, but I certainly don't tell things that aren't true." Jerry punctuated this pertinent speech with emphatic nods of her head, and, having said her say, walked on a little ahead of her friends, the picture of belligerence.

"Now, you've made Jerry angry, Mignon," laughed Susan Atwell.

Mignon merely lifted her thin shoulders. "I can't please every one. If I did, I should never please myself."

"I don't know what ails Jerry all of a sudden," commented Muriel to Marjorie. "She isn't usually so—so funny."

Again Marjorie kept her own counsel. She, alone, knew that the object of the rumor which Muriel and Mignon had started had failed. Ellen Seymour had gone frankly to headquarters with it, and Miss Archer had asked no questions. Marjorie wondered what these girls would say if they knew the truth. She did not like to criticize them, but were they truly honorable? For a moment she wished she had refused to play on the team with them. Muriel and Mignon, in particular, seemed so careless of other people's feelings.

Her sympathies were with Jerry, and quickening her pace she slipped her arm through that of the fat girl, saying, "Don't you think to-morrow's algebra lesson is hard?"

Jerry viewed her companion's smiling face rather sulkily. Then succumbing to the other's charm, she said in a mollified tone: "Of course it's hard. They're all hard. I know I shall never pass in algebra."

"Oh, yes, you will," was Marjorie's cheerful assurance. "It's my hardest study, too; but I'm going to pass my final examination in it. I've simply made up my mind that I must do it."

"Then I'll make up my mind to pass, too," announced Jerry, inspired by Marjorie's determined tones. "And, say, it would be splendid if we could do our lessons together sometimes. My mother likes me to bring my school friends home."

"So does mine," returned Marjorie, cordially. "She says home is the place for me to entertain my schoolmates. I hope you will come to see me soon. It's your turn first, you know. Oh, please pardon me a moment, I must speak to this girl!" The cause of this sudden exclamation was a young woman in a well-worn blue suit who was coming across the street directly ahead of them.

"Oh, Constance!" hailed Marjorie, "I have been looking for you. Stop a minute!" Marjorie stood waiting for her friend with eager face and outstretched hand. By this time the four other girls had come abreast of the trio and had passed them, Irma Linton being the only one of them who bowed to Constance. Jerry stood beside Marjorie for an instant, then walked on and overtook her chums.

"Please don't stop," begged Constance, her face expressing the liveliest worry. "Really, you mustn't try to be friends with me. I wish to take back my part of our compact. You've been chosen to play on the team, and those girls seem to like you. I can't stand in your way, and my friendship won't be worth anything to you, so just let's forget all we said the other day."

Marjorie stared hard at the other girl, the pathetic droop of whose lips looked for all the world like Mary's when things went wrong. "You don't mean that, and I won't give you up," she said with fine stubbornness. "I haven't time to talk about it now. I must catch up with those girls. Wait for me at our locker to-morrow noon, please, please."

With a hasty squeeze of Constance's hand, Marjorie raced on up the street to overtake her companions. They were so busily engaged in discussing her, however, that they did not hear her approach, and consequently did not lower their voices.

"I will not speak to her; I will not play with her on the team!" she heard Mignon La Salle sputter angrily.

"We certainly don't care to bother with her if she's going to take up with all sorts of low people." This loftily from Muriel, who was afraid to cross the French girl.

"My mother told me never to speak to any of those crazy Stevens persons," added Susan Atwell, with a toss of her curly head. "I don't care so very much for this Dean girl, either."

"Oh, you make me tired, the whole lot of you," cried Jerry, with angry contempt. "Marjorie Dean is nicer than all of you put together, and if she likes that little white-faced Stevens girl, then the girl is all right, even if her family were ragpickers. I'm ashamed of myself for being so silly as to listen to any of Mignon's complaints against her. You can do as you like, but if it's a case of being your friend or Marjorie's, then I guess I'd rather be hers."

"Thank you, Geraldine." Marjorie's quiet voice caused the party to turn, then exchange sheepish glances. "I don't wish you to quarrel over me," she went on. "I should like to be friends with all of you, but none of you can choose my friends for me any more than I can choose yours for you."

"You can't chum with us and be the friend of that Miss Stevens," muttered Mignon. "She is my enemy. Do you understand?"

"I am sorry to hear that," returned Marjorie, keeping her temper with difficulty, "but she is not mine. I like her. I shall stand up for her and be her friend as long as we go to Sanford High School. I am sorry to seem disagreeable, but I shouldn't feel the least bit true to myself if I were afraid to say what I think. This is my street. Good-bye."

Marjorie walked proudly away from the group. An instant and she heard the patter of running feet behind her.

"You can't get rid of us so easily," panted Geraldine Macy.

"I think you are right, Marjorie," said Irma Linton, quietly, putting out her hand. "I should like to be your friend."

And the dividing of the sextette of girls was the dividing of the freshman class of Sanford High School.

CHAPTER IX

A BITTER MOMENT

Marjorie went soberly up the steps of her home that afternoon. Her pleasure in making the team had been short-lived. She wondered if it would not be better to write her resignation. How could she bear to play on a team when three of the members had decided to drop her acquaintance? Still, they had not chosen her to play on the team; why, then, should she resign? She decided to consult her captain on the subject; then changed her mind. She would not trouble her mother with such petty grievances. This prejudice against Constance Stevens had originated wholly with Mignon La Salle. Perhaps the French girl would soon forget it, and it would die a natural death. Marjorie was not mortally hurt over the turn of the afternoon's affairs. She had not been so deeply impressed with the importance of Mignon and her friends that she failed to see their snobbish tendencies. She made mental exception of Jerry and Irma. She was secretly glad that they had declared for her. She liked Jerry's blunt independence and Irma's gentle, lovable personality. With the optimism of sixteen, she declined to worry over what had happened, and her report to her captain at the end of that troubled afternoon included only the pleasant events of the day.

When she went to school the next Monday morning she discovered that it did hurt, just a trifle, to be deliberately cut by the Picture Girl, and, instead of being greeted with Susan Atwell's dimpled smile, to receive an icy stare from that young woman, as, later in the morning, they passed each other in the corridor.

In some mysterious manner the story of the disagreement had been noised about the freshman class, with the result that Marjorie's acquaintance was eagerly sought by a number of freshmen whom she knew merely by sight, and that several girls, who had made it a point to smile and nod to her, now passed her, frigid and unsmiling.

As for the members of the little group Marjorie had watched so earnestly before she had been enrolled as a freshman at Sanford, they were now divided indeed. As the week progressed the "Terrible Trio," as Jerry had satirically named Mignon, Muriel and Susan, endeavored to make plain to whoever would listen to them that there was but one side to the story, namely, their side. Emulating Marjorie's example, Jerry and Irma had taken particular pains to be friendly with Constance Stevens. After an eloquent dissertation on friendship, delivered by Marjorie at their locker on the Monday morning following her disagreement with the other girls, Constance had shed a few happy tears and admitted that she had rather be "best friends" with Marjorie than anyone else in the world.

The hardest part of it all for Marjorie was her basketball practice. It was dreadful to be on speaking terms with only one girl on the team, Harriet Delaney, and she was not overly cordial. Marjorie tried to remember that Miss Randall had appointed her to her position, that the right to play was hers; but the unfriendly players made her nervous, and she lost her usual snap and daring. The second week's practice came, and she resolved to play up to her usual form, but, try as she might, she fell far short of the promise she had shown at the tryout. She also noted uneasily that, no matter how early she reported for practice, the team seemed always to be in the gymnasium before her and that one of the substitutes invariably held her position.

The freshmen had challenged the sophomores to play against them on the first Saturday afternoon in November. It was now the latter part of October and both teams were utilizing as much of their spare time as possible in preparing for the fray.

"Are you going to practice this afternoon?" whispered Geraldine Macy to Marjorie as they left the algebra class on Monday morning.

Marjorie nodded.

"Oh, dear," grumbled Jerry under her breath. "I wanted to talk to you about the Hallowe'en party."

"What Hallowe'en party?" asked Marjorie, opening her eyes.

"Haven't you your invitation?" It was Jerry's turn to look surprised.

"I don't even know what you're talking about."

Their entrance into the study hall put an end to the conversation. It was renewed at noon, however, when Jerry, Irma, Marjorie and Constance trooped out of the school building together, a seemingly contented quartet.

"Just imagine, girls," announced Jerry, excitedly. "Marjorie doesn't know a thing about the Hallowe'en party. She hasn't her invitation either. I think that's awfully queer."

"I haven't mine, but I know all about it," put in Constance Stevens, quietly.

"Who has charge of the invitations?" asked Marjorie.

"Miss Arnold. You'd better see her about yours to-day. Of course you both want to go."

"But what is it and where is it held?" questioned Marjorie.

"It's a big dance. Weston High School, that's the boys' school, gives a party to Sanford High on every Hallowe'en night. It's a town institution and as unchangeable as any law the Medes and Persians ever thought of making," informed Jerry.

"Oh, how splendid!" exclaimed Marjorie. "I should like to know some nice Sanford boys, and I love to dance!"

"Then you ought to meet my brother Hal," declared Jerry, solemnly, "for he's the nicest, handsomest, best boy I know."

"Wait until you see the Crane," laughed Irma Linton. "He's the tallest boy in high school. He's six feet two inches now. They say he hasn't stopped growing, either, and he is awfully thin. That's why the boys call him the 'Crane.' He doesn't mind it a bit. His real name is Sherman Norwood, but no one ever calls him that except the teachers."

During the rest of the walk home the coming dance was the sole subject under discussion. Yes, the girls wore evening gowns, if they had them. Lots of girls wore their best summer dresses. The leading caterer of Sanford always had charge of the refreshments and the boys paid the bills. There was a real orchestra, too. Of course all the teachers were there, but the pokey ones went home early and the jolly ones, like Miss Flint and Miss Atkins, stayed until the last dance.

There were countless other questions to ask, but the luncheon hour was too short to admit of any lingering on the corner.

"I wish we had more time to talk," sighed Marjorie, reluctantly, as she came to her street. "I'd love to hear more about the dance."

"We'll tell you all there is to tell after school," promised Jerry. "Oh, no, we can't either. You'll have to go to that old basketball practice. What a nuisance it is. And to think you have to play on the team with Mignon, Muriel and Susan, after the way they've treated you. Why don't you resign?"

"I don't believe I'll play next term," said Marjorie, slowly, "but I feel as though I ought to stay on the team for the rest of this term. Our game with the sophomores is set for two weeks from to-morrow; then, I believe we are to play against two teams from nearby towns. It wouldn't be fair to leave the team now, after having practiced with it."

"I don't believe I'd bother my head much about that part of it," sniffed Jerry, "I'd just quit."

"No, you wouldn't, Geraldine Macy," laughed Irma. "You might grumble, but you wouldn't be so hateful."

"You don't know how hateful I can be," warned Jerry. "Some other girls are likely to find out, though."

"Good-bye. I must not stop here another second," declared Marjorie.

"Good-bye!" floated after her as she walked rapidly toward home.

"How goes it, Lieutenant?" asked her father, who, with her mother, was already seated at the table as she entered the dining-room.

"Pretty well, thank you, General," she replied, touching her hand to her curly head.

"I haven't heard you say a word about school for at least a week, my dear," commented her mother. "Has the novelty of Sanford High worn off so soon?"

"No, indeed, Captain," returned Marjorie, earnestly. "I'm finding out new things every day." She did not add that some of the "new things" had not been agreeable, nor did she volunteer any further information concerning her school. This touch of reticence on the part of her usually talkative daughter caused her mother to look at her searchingly and wonder if Marjorie had something on her mind which in due season would be brought to light. The subject of the dance returning to the young girl's thoughts, she began at once to talk of it, and her enthusiastic description of the coming affair served to allay her mother's vague impression that Marjorie was not quite happy, and she entered into the important discussion of what her daughter should wear with that unselfish interest belonging only to a mother.

When Marjorie returned to school that afternoon she felt happier than she had been since her advent into Sanford High School. The thought of the coming dance brought with it a delightful thrill of anticipation. She had always had such good times at the school dances given by her boy and her girl chums of B——. She hoped she would enjoy this Hallowe'en frolic. She wondered if the "Terrible Trio" would be there. She smiled over Jerry's appropriate appellation, then frowned at herself for countenancing it. Good soldiers didn't indulge in personalities.

That afternoon she found it hard, however, to concentrate her thoughts on her studies, and when Miss Atkins asked her on what day the Pilgrim Fathers landed in America, she absent-mindedly replied "Hallowe'en," to the great joy of her class. During her physiology hour she managed to keep strictly to the subject; but she was impatient for the afternoon to pass so that she could go to Miss Arnold for her invitation.

Her eyes sparkled, however, when, on returning to the study hall, she saw lying on her desk a square white envelope addressed to her.

"Oh, here it is," she thought delightedly. "I'm so glad. I wonder if Constance has hers."

She tore open the end of the envelope with eager fingers and drew out a folded sheet of note paper. But the light died out of her face as she read:

"My dear Miss Dean:

"For some time the members of the freshman team have been dissatisfied with your playing, and have repeatedly urged me to allow Miss Thornton to play in your position on the team. Not wishing to seem unfair, Miss Randall and I watched your work at practice Wednesday afternoon and agreed that the requested change would be best. As manager of the freshmen team, their welfare must ever be my first consideration. I therefore feel no hesitation in asking you for your resignation from the team.

"Yours sincerely,

"Marcia Arnold."

A sigh of humiliation that was half a sob rose to Marjorie's lips. Her chin quivered ominously. Suddenly a dreadful thought flashed across her brain. Suppose Mignon and the others were watching her to see how she received the bad news. Marjorie's desire to cry left her. She leaned back in her seat and assumed an air of indifference far removed from her real state of mind. Then she calmly refolded the letter and placed it in its envelope with the impassivity of a young sphinx.

Later that afternoon, as Mignon La Salle strolled out of school between her two satellites, Susan and Muriel, she was heard to declare with disappointed peevishness that that priggish Miss Dean was either too stupid to resent or too thick-skinned to feel a plain out-and-out snub.

CHAPTER X

A BLUE GOWN AND A SOLEMN RESOLVE

The next day in school was a particularly trying one for poor Marjorie. It was decidedly hard for the sore-hearted little freshman to believe that Miss Arnold's motive in asking her to resign from the team had been purely disinterested. She was reasonably sure that she had Mignon to blame for the humiliation. Jerry Macy had told her of Miss Arnold's respect for Mignon's father's money, and that Miss Archer's thin-lipped, austere-looking secretary was one of the French girl's most devoted followers.

The wave of dislike which had swept over Marjorie upon first beholding Marcia Arnold had, as the days passed, intensified rather than lessened. Jerry, too, could not endure the secretary. "I never could bear her," she had confided to Marjorie. "I'm glad she's a junior. I'll have two years of comfort after she's gone. I suppose she deserves a lot of credit for keeping up in her studies and earning money as a secretary at the same time, but I'd rather have a nice wriggly snake, or a cheerful crocodile for a friend if it comes to a choice."

Marjorie was equally certain that Miss Arnold did not like her. She had had occasion to ask the secretary several questions and the latter's manner of answering had been curt, almost to rudeness. The desired resignation was yet to be written. Marjorie had purposely delayed writing it until the last hour of the afternoon session. She wished to think before writing. It took her the greater part of the hour to compose it, although, when it was finally copied on a sheet of note paper she had brought to school for that purpose, it covered little more than one side of the sheet.

While she was addressing it for mailing, she suddenly remembered that she had not yet asked Miss Arnold for her Hallowe'en invitation. Should she hand the secretary her resignation instead of mailing it? She decided that the more dignified course would be to mail it. As to the invitation for the dance, she was entitled to it; therefore she was not afraid to demand it. She wondered if Constance had received hers, and, when her new friend returned from class, Marjorie managed to catch her eye and question her by means of a sign language known only to schoolgirls. A vigorous shake of Constance's fair head brought forth more signs, which, when school was dismissed, resulted in a determined march upon Miss Archer's office by the two friends, reinforced by Jerry and Irma, who had managed to join Marjorie and Constance in the corridor.

"That's just why we waited," announced Jerry, wagging her head emphatically when Marjorie explained her mission. "We wondered if she'd given them to you. You let me do the talking. She won't have a word to say when I'm through."

"Hush, Jerry!" cautioned Irma. "She'll hear you."

They were now entering Miss Archer's living-room office. Marcia Arnold, who was seated before her desk, intent on the book she held in her hand, raised her eyes and regarded the quartette with a displeased frown. Then she addressed them in peremptory tones.

"Please make less noise, girls. Your voices can be plainly heard in Miss Archer's office and she is too busy now to be disturbed." This last with a view to discouraging any attempt on their part to see the principal.

"We didn't come to see Miss Archer," was Geraldine Macy's calm retort. "We came to see you about Miss Dean's and Miss Stevens' invitations for the dance. They haven't received them."

"I know nothing whatever about them," snapped Miss Arnold, picking up her book as a sign of dismissal.

"You ought to know. The invitations were given to you by the boys' committee," was Jerry's pertinent reminder. "You sent them the list of names, didn't you? Perhaps you accidentally left out these two names."

This was a malicious afterthought on Jerry's part, but it had a potent effect on Marcia Arnold. A tide of red rose to her sallow face. For a second her eyes wavered from the four pairs searchingly upon her. Then she answered with elaborate carelessness: "It is just possible that these two names have been omitted. I will go over my list and see."

"Yes, do," advised Jerry, laconically. Then she slyly added: "It seems funny, doesn't it, that when 'D' and 'S' are so far apart on the alphabetical list, they should both happen to be overlooked? If the girls don't receive their invitations by to-morrow night I'll speak to my brother about it. He's the president of the junior class, you know, and he'll take it up with the committee. Come on, girls."

The three young women obediently following her, Jerry marched from the room with the air of a conqueror. True to her prediction, Marcia Arnold had found nothing to say to the stout girl's parting shot.

"There really wasn't much use in our going. I'm afraid we weren't very brave. We shouldn't have stood like wooden images and let you fight our battles, Jerry. It was awfully dear in you, but I do hope Miss Arnold won't think Constance and I are babies," demurred Marjorie.

"What do you care what she thinks as long as she hunts up your invitations?" asked Jerry, with superb contempt. "What she thinks will never hurt either of you."

The belated invitations were delivered to the two freshmen by Miss Arnold herself the next day, greatly to Jerry's satisfaction.

"I saw her give them to you, girls," she whispered to Marjorie on the way to the English class. "She looked mad as a hatter, too. She thought she'd hold back your invitations until the last minute; then maybe you would get mad and not go to the dance."

"But why should she wish to keep us from going?" asked Marjorie, wonderingly.

"Ask Mignon," was Jerry's enigmatical answer. "Very likely she knows more about it than anyone else."

Marjorie found no chance for conversation with Constance until they met in French class. Even then she had only time to say, "Be sure to wait for me this noon," before Professor Fontaine called his class to order and attacked the advance lesson with his usual Latin ardor.

Constance was first at their locker. She had already put on her own hat and coat and was holding Marjorie's for her, when her friend arrived.

"What are you going to wear, Constance?" asked Marjorie, as she put on her coat and hat.

"I'm not going," was the brief answer.

"Not going!" Marjorie stared hard at her friend. Was Constance hurt because she had not received her invitation? Then she went on, eagerly apologetic: "It wasn't the Weston boys' fault that we didn't get our invitations when the others received theirs. They didn't intend to leave us out, even though they only knew our names."

"It's not that." Constance's voice trembled a little. "I—I—well, I haven't a dress fit to wear!" Her pale cheeks grew pink with shame as she burst forth with this confession of poverty. "This blue suit and three house dresses are all the clothes I have in the world. Don't say you feel sorry for me. I shall hate you if you do. I sha'n't always be poor. Some day," her eyes grew dreamy, "I'll have all sorts of lovely clothes. When I am a——" She stopped abruptly, then said in her usual half-sullen tones, "I can't go, so don't ask me."

Marjorie looked curiously at this strange girl. The longer she knew Constance the better she liked her, but she did not in the least understand her. Suddenly a bright idea popped into her head. "I'm so sorry you can't go to the dance," she commented, then promptly dropped the subject. When she left Constance, however, she remarked innocently: "Don't forget, you are coming home with me to-night. Don't say you can't. You promised, you know."

"I will come," promised Constance, brightening. "Good-bye."

The moment Marjorie reached home she made a dash for her room and going to her closet, emerged a moment afterward with an immense white pasteboard box in her arms. Stopping only long enough to drop her wraps on her bed she ran downstairs and burst into the dining-room with: "I have found her, Mother. I've found the girl this was made for."

"What is all this commotion about, Lieutenant?" asked her father, teasingly. "Are we about to be attacked by the enemy? Salute your superior officers and then state your case. Discipline must be preserved at all costs in the army. Is it a requisition for new uniforms? You soldiers are dreadfully hard on your clothes. Or is the post about to move and is that a packing case?"

Marjorie made a most unsoldierlike rush for him and, throwing her arms about his neck, kissed his cheek. "You are a great big tease, and I choose to salute you this way." Then she kissed her mother, saying: "I've the loveliest plan, Captain. I'm sure that this dress will fit Constance. She says she won't go to the school dance because she has no pretty gown to wear. May I give her this darling blue one?" She opened the box and drew forth a dainty frock of pale blue chiffon over silk. The chiffon was caught up here and there with tiny clusters of pinky-white rosebuds. The round neck was just low enough to show to advantage a white girlish throat, while the soft, fluffy sleeves reached barely to the elbows. It was a particularly beautiful and appropriate frock for a young girl.

"You see, General," explained Marjorie, "Aunt Mary sent this to me when I graduated from grammar school. She hadn't seen me for two years and didn't know I had grown so fast. She bought it ready made in one of the New York stores. It was too short and too tight for me and to make it over meant simply to spoil it. It was so sweet in her to send it that when I wrote my thank you to her I couldn't bear to tell her that it didn't fit, so I kept it just to look at. I didn't really need it, for, thanks to you and mother, I have plenty of others. Don't you think I ought to make someone else happy when I have the chance? It is right to share one's spoils with a comrade, isn't it?"

Her father looked lovingly at the pretty, earnest face of his daughter as she stood holding up the filmy gown, her eyes bright with unselfish purpose. "I am very glad my little girl is so thoughtful of others," he said. "Whatever your captain says is law. How about it, Captain?" His wife and he exchanged glances.

"You may give your friend the dress if you like, dear," consented Mrs. Dean, "if you think she will accept it."

"That's just the point, Captain," returned Marjorie. "You know you said I could bring Constance home for dinner to-night, and she is coming. Perhaps we can think of some nice way to give it to her while she is here."

Marjorie carefully replaced the gown in its box and ran upstairs with it. She returned with her hat and coat on her arm, and hanging them on the hall rack hastened to eat her luncheon.

All afternoon she puzzled as to how she might best offer Constance the gown. When the four girls strolled homeward together after school she had still not thought of a way. Jerry and Irma held forth, at length, with true schoolgirl eloquence, upon the subject of their gowns. Constance listened gravely without comment. Her small, impassive face showed no sign of her hopeless longing for the pretty things she had never possessed.

Once inside the Dean's pleasant home, a flash of appreciation routed her impassivity as Marjorie conducted her into the comfortable living-room where Mrs. Dean sat reading, and her face softened under the spell of the older woman's gentle greeting.

"I am pleased to know you, Constance," said Mrs. Dean, offering her hand. "I have been expecting you for some time. Now that I have seen you I will say that you do look very much like Marjorie's friend Mary." She did not add that this girl's face lacked the good-natured, happy expression that so perfectly matched Mary Raymond's sunny curls. Yet she noted that the blue eyes met hers openly and frankly, and that there was an undeniable air of sincerity and truth about Constance which caused one instinctively to trust her.

To the formerly friendless girl who had never before been invited to the home of a Sanford girl, the evening passed like a dream. Under the genial atmosphere of the Dean household, her reserve melted and before dinner was over she had forgotten all about herself and was laughing merrily with Marjorie over Mr. Dean's nonsense. After dinner Mrs. Dean played on the piano and Constance, who knew how to dance was initiated into the mysteries of several new steps which were favorites of the Franklin girls, and later the two girls spent a happy hour in Marjorie's room with her books, of which she had a large collection.

"Oh, dear," sighed Constance, as she glanced at the clock on the chiffonier. "It is ten o'clock. I must go."

"Wait a few minutes," requested Marjorie. "I have something to show you, but I must see mother for a minute first. Please excuse me. I'll be back directly."

"Mother," Marjorie hurried into the living-room. "Have you thought of a way? Constance is going home, and it's now or never."

"Suppose you give it to her by yourself," suggested her mother. "I am afraid my presence will embarrass her and then she will surely refuse."

Marjorie stood eyeing her mother uncertainly. Then she laughed. "I know the easiest way in the world," she declared, and was gone.

When she entered the room Constance was kneeling interestedly before the book-shelves. "You have the 'Jungle Books,' haven't you? Don't you love them?"

"Yes," laughed Marjorie. "Mary and I read them together. I always called myself 'Bagheera' the black panther, and she always called herself 'Mogli, the man-cub.' We used to write notes to each other sometimes in the language of the jungle."

"How funny," smiled Constance. Her gaze intent upon the books, she did not notice that Marjorie had stepped to her closet, returning to her bed with a cloud of pink over her arm. Next she opened a big box and laid a cloud of blue beside the one of pink. "Constance, come here a minute," she said.

Constance sprang up obediently. Her glance fell upon the bed and she gave a little startled, admiring "Oh!"

Marjorie linked her arm in that of her friend and drew her up to the bed. "This gown," she pointed to the pink one, "is mine, and this one," she withdrew her arm, and lifting the blue cloud held it out to Constance, "is yours."

The Mary girl drew back sharply. "I don't know what you mean," she muttered. "Please don't make fun of me."

"I'm not making fun of you. It's your very own, and after I tell you all about it you'll see just why it happens to be yours."

Seated on the edge of the bed beside Marjorie, the wonderful blue gown on her lap, the girl who had never owned a party dress before heard the story of how it happened to be hers. At first she steadily refused its acceptance, but in the end wily Marjorie persuaded her to "just try it on," and when she saw herself, for the first time in her poverty-stricken young life, wearing a real evening gown that glimpsed her unusually white neck and arms she wavered. So intent was she upon examining her reflection that she did not notice Marjorie had slipped from the room, returning with a pair of blue silk stockings and satin slippers to match. "These go with it," she announced.

"Oh—I—can't," faltered Constance, making a move toward unhooking the frock.

"Of course you can." Marjorie deposited the stockings and slippers on the foot of her bed and going over to Constance put both arms around her. "You are going to have this dress because mother and I want you to. I can't possibly wear it myself, and it's a shame to lay it away in the closet until it is all out of style. Please, please take it. You simply must, for I won't go to the dance unless you do, and you know how dreadfully I should hate to miss it. I mean what I say, too."

"I'll take it," said Constance, slowly.

Suddenly she slipped from Marjorie's encircling arm and leaned against the chiffonier, covering her face with her hands.

"Constance!" Marjorie cried out in surprise. "You mustn't cry."

"I—can't—help—it." The words came brokenly. "Ever since I was little I've dreamed about a blue dress like this. You—are—too—good—to—me. Nobody—was—ever—good to me before."

It was a quarter to eleven o'clock before Constance, her tears dried, her face beaming with a new expression of happiness, left the Deans' house, accompanied by Mr. Dean, who had come in shortly before ten o'clock and insisted on seeing her safely home.

Later, as she prepared for bed in her bare little room she could not help wondering why Marjorie had desired her for a best friend, and had clung to her in spite of the displeasure of certain other girls. She wondered, too, if there were any way in which she might show Marjorie her affection and gratitude, and she made a solemn resolve that if that time came she would prove herself worthy of Marjorie Dean's friendship.

CHAPTER XI

THE HALLOWE'EN DANCE

Saturday dawned as inauspiciously as any other day in the week, but to the high school boys and girls of the little city of Sanford it was a day set apart. Aside from commencement, the great event of their high school year was about to take place.

As early as eight o'clock that morning the decorating committee of Weston High School was up and laboring manfully at the task of turning Weston's big gymnasium into a veritable bower of beauty, which should, in due season, draw forth plenty of admiring "Ohs!" and "Ahs!" from their gentle guests. For three days the committee had been borrowing, with lavish promises of safe return, as many cushions, draperies, chairs, divans and various other articles calculated to fitly adorn the ballroom, as their families and friends confidingly allowed them to carry off.

Their progress along this line had been painstakingly watched by numerous pairs of sharp, young eyes, and the report had gone forth among the girls that this particular Hallowe'en party was going to be "the nicest dance the boys had ever given."

To Marjorie Dean, however, the event promised more than the usual interest. It was to be her first opportunity of entering into the social life of the boys and girls of Sanford. In B—— she had numbered many stanch friends among the young men of Lafayette High School, but she had lived in Sanford for, what seemed to her, a very long time and had not met a single Weston boy. Jerry had promised to introduce Marjorie to her brother and to the tall, fair-haired youth known as the Crane, but so far the young people had not been thrown together. Marjorie had no silly, sentimental ideas in her curly brown head about boys. From early childhood she had been allowed to play with them. She was fond of their games and had always evinced far more interest in marbles, tops and even baseball than she had in dolls. Still, at sixteen, she was not a hoyden nor a tomboy, but a merry, light-hearted girl with a strong, healthy body and a feeling of comradeship toward boys in general which was to carry her far in her later life.

At the time she had given Constance the blue gown she had also gained her friend's rather reluctant consent to come to dinner at the Deans' on the great night and dress with her for the dance. Marjorie attributed Constance's hesitation to shyness. Always reticent regarding her home life, Constance, aside from her one outburst relating to her family on the day when she had advised Marjorie against her friendship, had said little or nothing further of her home. So Marjorie did not know that it was not a matter of shyness, but rather a question of who would keep house and get the supper while she was out enjoying herself, that caused Constance to demur before accepting the invitation. Then she remembered that Hallowe'en came on Saturday and decided that she could manage after all.

The momentous Saturday dawned clear and cold, with just the suspicion of a fall tang to the air. It was a busy day for the Weston boys, and when at four o'clock the last garland of green had been twined about the gymnasium posts and the gallery railing, while the last flag had been painstakingly hung at the proper angle, the dozen or more of young men who formed the decorating committee viewed their work with boyish pride.

"It looks bully," shouted an enthusiastic freshman, with a sweep of his arm which was intended to include the whole room. "If the girls aren't suited with this, they won't be invited over here again in a hurry."

"Hear him rave!" sadly commented a sophomore. "It takes a freshman to fall all over himself."

"That's because we are young and have more enthusiasm," retorted the freshman, his freckled face alive with an impish grin.

 "Desist from your squabbles

And join in the waltz,"

caroled an extremely tall, thin youth, pirouetting on his toes, and waving a long trail of ground pine about his head in true première danseuse fashion.

There was a shout of laughter from the boys at this burst of terpsichorean art. The tall youth pranced and whirled the length of the gymnasium and back, ending his performance with a swift, high kick and a bow that bade fair to dislocate his spine.

"Did I hear someone laugh?" he asked severely, drawing down his face with such an indescribably funny expression that the laughter broke forth afresh. "It is evident that you don't appreciate my rare ability as a dancer."

"You mean as a grasshopper," jeered the freckle-faced youth.

"Exactly. No, I don't either. How dare you insult me?" He made a lengthy lunge toward the freshman, who promptly dodged behind a tall, good-looking young man who had at that moment joined the group.

The lunging youth brought up short with, "Hello, Hal, I thought you had gone."

"So I had. Got halfway home and found I'd left my pocketknife here. Maybe I didn't hotfoot it back though. Hope the girls will like the looks of things." He cast approving eyes about the transformed gymnasium. "Jerry's been raving to me ever since school began about her new friend, Marjorie Dean. Have you met her? I understand she is coming to-night."

"Not I, I can't tell one of those girls from another," grumbled the Crane. "You know just how much I like girls. I don't mind helping get ready for this business, but I'd rather take a licking than come back here to-night. You'll see me vanishing around the corner and out of here at the very first chance. Girls are an awful nuisance anyway."

"Nothing like true chivalry," murmured the freckle-faced freshman. An instant later he was sprinting down the gymnasium as fast as his short legs could carry him, the Crane in hot pursuit.

"Cut it out, fellows," laughed Harold Macy. "You'll upset something or other, and then, look out."

"If we do it will be the Crane's fault," came plaintively from the freckle-faced freshman, as he dodged his pursuer with an agility born of long practice. "I don't see why he wants to chase me. I merely made a simple remark."

"Now that you've owned up to its being simple I'll let you off this time," declared the Crane, magnanimously, "but see that it doesn't happen again."

"I will," was the glib promise. "I'm sorry I said you were a grasshopper. You look more like a giraffe."

Then he made a hurried exit through a nearby side door, leaving the Crane to vow dire vengeance the next time he ventured within reach.

A little further loitering and the group of boys broke up, and, leaving the gymnasium, went home to get ready for the evening's fun and be back in good season to help receive their guests.

There were two guests, however, who dressed for the party with entirely different emotions. To Constance it was the most wonderful night of her life. She stole frequent, half-startled glances at her blue satin-shod feet and even pinched a fold of her chiffon gown between her fingers to feel if it were real. Mrs. Dean had arranged the girl's fair curling hair in precisely the same fashion that Mary Raymond wore hers, and when she had been hooked into the precious gown, with its exquisite little sprays of rosebuds, she thought she knew just how poor, lowly Cinderella felt when the fairy godmother touched her with her wand. While she was being dressed she said little, yet Marjorie and her mother knew by the happy light that crowded the wistful look quite out of her expressive eyes that their guest was too deeply appreciative for words.

Marjorie, who looked radiantly pretty in her frock of pink silk with its overdress of delicate pink net, welcomed the dance with all the enthusiasm of one who was heartily glad to get in touch with the social side of her school life. She had forgotten for the moment that certain girls in the freshman class had turned against her; that she was no longer a member of the freshman basketball team. She remembered only that it seemed ages since she had attended a party and she hoped fervently that someone would ask her to dance.

Jerry and Irma had arranged to call for Marjorie and Constance, as the quartette were to use the Macys' limousine. When the automobile stopped before the house, Jerry insisted on getting out and running into the house to see her friends' gowns. Irma followed her, a smile of good-natured tolerance on her placid face.

"Jerry couldn't wait to see your dresses," she said, then exclaimed in wonder: "How lovely you look, Constance, and what a perfectly sweet gown!"

Constance colored to the tips of her small ears. Jerry, too, began voicing loud approval, and when, after having stood in line and been inspected by Mrs. Dean, the four girls piled into the limousine, Constance was overcome with the peculiar sensation of experiencing too much happiness. She felt that it could not possibly last.

The gymnasium was fairly well filled when they entered and by half past eight o'clock the majority of the guests had arrived. Hardly had they deposited their scarfs in the dressing-room and administered last judicious pats to straying fluffy locks of hair when Jerry, who had disappeared the moment they reached the dressing-room, came hurrying back with the information that Hal was waiting outside to do the honors. "You'd better hurry out and console the Crane, Irma," she added slyly. "He looks about ten feet tall in his evening clothes and perfectly miserable."

Following in Jerry's wake Marjorie stepped into the gaily decorated room and the next instant was shaking hands with handsome Hal Macy, the most popular fellow in Weston High. As the brown eyes met the frank manly gaze of the gray, there passed between the two young people a vivid flash of liking and comradeship that was later to develop into a stanch and beautiful friendship.

"I am so glad to know you," said Marjorie, earnestly. "I am very fond of your sister."

"I am sure we shall be friends," declared Hal Macy. Involuntarily he put out his hand. Marjorie's hand met it, and thus began the friendship between Marjorie Dean and Hal Macy.

CHAPTER XII

ON THE FIRING LINE

Introductions followed thick and fast. More than one pair of boyish eyes had been centered approvingly on the girls that "Macy" was "rushing," and he was soon besieged with gentle reminders not to be stingy, but to give someone else a chance.

When the enlivening strains of a popular dance began, Hal Macy pointed significantly to his name on Marjorie's card. She nodded happily then glanced quickly about to see if Constance had a partner. Surely enough, she was just about to dance off with a rather tall, slender lad, whose dark, sensitive face, heavy-browed, black-lashed eyes of intense blue and straight-lipped, sensitive mouth caused her to say impulsively, "Oh, who is that nice-looking boy dancing with Constance?"

Hal glanced after the two graceful, gliding figures. "That's Lawrence Armitage. He's one of the best fellows in school and my chum. You ought to hear him play on the violin. He's going to Europe to study when he finishes high school."

"How interesting," commented Marjorie as they joined the dancers. Then, as Mignon La Salle, wearing an elaborate apricot satin frock, flashed by them on the arm of a rather stout boy, with a disagreeable face, Marjorie suddenly remembered the existence of Mignon, Muriel and Susan. Her eyes began an eager search for the Picture Girl. Muriel was sure to look pretty in evening dress. Mignon's frock made her look older, she decided. She soon spied Muriel, whose gown of white lace was vastly becoming. So was Susan Atwell's dress of old rose and silver. She wondered a trifle wickedly if they had not been surprised to see Constance blossom out in such brave attire. Then she put the thought aside as unworthy and determined to remember only the good time she was having.

After each dance the four friends managed to meet and compare notes before they were off again with their next partners, and as the party progressed it became noticeable that there were no wallflowers in that particular group.

"What do you think of that Stevens girl to-night, Mignon?" inquired Susan Atwell as she and the French girl stood together for a moment between dances.

Mignon's elfish eyes gleamed angrily. "I think such beggars as she ought never to be allowed to come to our parties. Goodness knows where she borrowed that dress. Perhaps she didn't borrow it." She raised her shoulders significantly. "If Laurie Armitage knew what a low, disreputable family she has, I don't think he'd waste his time with her."

"Did Laurie ask you to dance to-night?" asked Susan inquisitively.

But with a muttered, "I want to speak to Marcia," Mignon flounced off without answering Susan's question, and the latter confided to Muriel afterward that Mignon was mad as anything because Laurie hadn't noticed her, but was trailing about after Miss Nobody Stevens.

Completely unaware that she was adding to the French girl's list of grievances, Constance had danced to her heart's content, quite positive in her own mind that she had never met a more delightful boy than Lawrence Armitage, and that never before had she so greatly enjoyed herself. And now the wonderful party was almost over. She examined her card to see with whom she had the next dance. Then her glance straying down, she noticed that a bit of the tiny plaiting at the bottom of her chiffon skirt had become loose and was hanging. Fearful of a fall, she hurried toward the dressing-room. She would have the maid take a stitch or two in it.

But the maid was not in the room.

A solitary figure in an apricot gown stood before the mirror, lingered for a moment after Constance entered, then glided noiselessly out. Evincing no sign of having seen Mignon, Constance began a diligent hunt for a needle and thread. Failing to find them, she fastened the loose bit of plaiting with a pin and hurried out into the gymnasium. Her next dance was with Lawrence Armitage. She must not miss it.

To her surprise Mignon re-entered the dressing-room as she left it. Constance quickly made her way toward the corner which her friends had selected as their headquarters.

"I tore the plaiting of my dress," she said ruefully to Marjorie. "I couldn't find the maid or a needle, so I had to pin it. I'm awfully sorry. I don't know how it happened."

"That's nothing," returned Marjorie, cheerfully. "I have a great long tear in my sleeve. Someone caught hold of it in Paul Jones, and away it went. Don't look so guilty over a little thing like that."

"You don't——" began Constance, but she never finished.

A tense little figure clad in apricot satin confronted her, crying out in tones too plainly audible to those standing near, "Where is my bracelet? What have you done with it?"

Constance stared at her accuser in stupefied amazement. Her friends, too, were for the moment speechless.

"Answer me!" commanded Mignon. "I left it on the table in the dressing-room. You were the only one in there at the time. When I remembered and came back for it you were just leaving, but the bracelet was gone. No one else except you could have taken it."

Still Constance continued to stare in horror at the French girl. She tried to speak, but the words would not come. Attracted by Mignon's shrill tones, the dancers began to gather about the two girls. It was Marjorie who came to her friend's defense.

Even as a wee girl Marjorie Dean had possessed a temper. It was not an ordinary temper. It was not easily aroused, but when once awakened it shook her small body with intense fury and the object of her rage was likely to remember her outburst forever after. Knowing it to be her greatest fault, she had striven diligently to conquer it and it burst forth only at rare intervals. To-night, however, the French girl's heartless denunciation of Constance during a moment of happiness was too monstrous to be borne. In a voice shaking with indignation she turned to those surrounding her and said, "Will you please go on dancing? I have something to say to Miss La Salle."

They scattered as if by magic, leaving Marjorie facing Mignon, her arm about Constance, her face a white mask, her eyes flaming with scorn. Then she began in low, even tones:

"I forbid you to say another word either to or about my friend Constance Stevens. She has not taken your bracelet. She knows nothing about it. I will answer for her as I would for myself. You have accused her of this because you wish to disgrace her in the eyes of her friends and schoolmates. I am not at all sure that you have lost it, but I am very sure that Miss Stevens hasn't seen it. And now I hope I shall never be called upon to speak to you again, for you are the cruelest, most contemptible girl I have ever known; but, if I hear anything further of this, I will take you to Miss Archer, to the Board of Education, if necessary, and make you retract every word. Come on, Constance."

With her arm still encircling the now weeping girl, Marjorie made her way to the dressing-room. Jerry followed her within the next five minutes.

"The car's here," she announced briefly. "Hal and Laurie and the Crane are going home with us."

"Don't you cry, Constance," she soothed, patting the curly, golden head. "Mignon made a goose of herself to-night. The boys are all disgusted, and everyone knows she was making a fuss over nothing. You did exactly right, too, Marjorie, when you sent us all about our business. I'm sorry it happened, but you remember what I tell you, Mignon has hurt herself a great deal more than she has hurt you."

CHAPTER XIII

A PITCHED BATTLE

After the echoes of the dance had died away, basketball received a new impetus that brought it to the fore with a bound. With the renewed interest in the coming game was also noised about the report that "Miss Dean wasn't on the team any longer," and in some unknown fashion the news that she had been "asked" to resign had also gone the round of the study hall. The upper class girls were not particularly interested either in Marjorie or her affairs. She had not lived in Sanford long enough to become well-known to them, and as a rule the juniors and seniors left the bringing up of the freshmen to their sophomore sisters. The sophomores were too much absorbed in the progress of their own team to trouble themselves greatly over what was happening in the freshman organization. If Muriel or Mignon had resigned, then there would have been good cause for predicting an easy victory, for both girls were considered formidable opponents; but Marjorie was new material, untried and unproven.

It was in the freshman class, however, that comment ran rife. Since the night of the Weston dance the class had been almost equally divided. A little less than half the girls had either openly or by friendly smiles and nods declared in favor of Marjorie and her friends. The remaining members of the class, with a few neutral exceptions, were apparently devoted to the French girl and Muriel. Among their adherents they also counted Miss Merton, who took no pains to conceal her open dislike for Marjorie, and Marcia Arnold, who even went so far as to try to explain the situation to Miss Archer and was sternly reminded that the principal would take no part in the private differences of her girls unless they had something to do with breaking the rules of the school.

The days immediately preceding the game were not cheerful ones for Marjorie. She was still unhappy over her unjust dismissal from the team, and she wondered if it had been much talked of among her classmates. At home she had announced offhandedly her resignation from the team and her mother had asked no questions.

Mignon was greatly disturbed and displeased with the advent of Marjorie Dean into Sanford High School. Young as she was, she was very shrewd, and she at once foresaw in Marjorie's pretty face and attractive personality a rival power. To be sure, Marjorie's father was not so rich as her own, but it could not be denied that the Deans lived in a big house on Maple avenue, that Marjorie wore "perfectly lovely" clothes and had plenty of pocket money. In the beginning she had decided that it would be better to make friends with her, but Marjorie's sturdy defense of Constance and utter disregard for Mignon's significant warning had shown her plainly that she could not influence the other girl to do what she considered an unworthy act. Therefore, she had secretly determined to make matters as disagreeable as lay within her power for the two girls during her freshman year. Still she was obliged to admit to herself that her next move would have to be planned and carried out with more discretion.

And now it was the Friday before the much-heralded basketball game which was to be played between the sophomores and the freshmen, and the merits and shortcomings of the respective organizations were being eagerly discussed throughout the school. The game was to be called at half-past two o'clock on Saturday afternoon, and from all accounts there was to be no lack of spectators.

"I wouldn't for anything miss that game to-morrow!" exclaimed Jerry Macy, as she and Constance and Marjorie came down the steps of the school together. "I hope the freshmen get the worst whitewashing that any team in this school has ever had, too," she added, with a deliberate air of spite.

"You mustn't say that, Jerry," returned Marjorie, a faint color rising to her cheeks. "You must not let my grievances affect your loyalty to your class."

"Do you mean to say that you want that horrid Mignon La Salle and her crowd to win the game, and then go around crowing that it was all because they put you out of the team? You needn't look so as though you didn't believe me. You mark my word, if they win you'll find out that they'll do just as I say. Freshman or no freshman, I'd rather see that nice Ellen Seymour's team win any day."

"So would I," echoed Constance, her face darkening with the remembrance of her own wrongs at Mignon's hands.

Marjorie was silent for a moment. She knew that Jerry's outburst rose from pure devotion to her friends, and she could not blame Constance for her hostile spirit. Still, was it right to allow personal grudges to warp one's loyalty to one's class? If the record of their class read badly at the end of their freshman year, whose fault would it be? She had fought it all out with herself on the day she wrote her resignation, and had wisely determined, then, not to allow it to spoil her year.

"I know how you girls feel about this," she said slowly. "I felt the same way until after I had written my resignation. While I was writing I kept hoping that the team would lose and be sorry they had put someone else in my place. Then it just came to me all of a sudden that a good soldier wouldn't be a traitor to his country even if he were reduced in rank or had something happen unpleasant to him in his camp."

She stopped and looked embarrassed. She had forgotten that the girls could not possibly know what she meant. She had never told any one in Sanford High School about the pretty soldier play which she and Mary had carried on for so long. It was one of the little intimate details of her life which she preferred to keep to herself. Should she explain? Jerry's impatient retort made it unnecessary.

"The only traitor I know anything about is Mignon," she flung back, failing to grasp the significance of Marjorie's comparison.

Constance, however, had flashed a curious glance at her friend, saying nothing. When Geraldine had nodded good-bye at her street, and the two were alone, she asked: "What did you mean by comparing yourself to a soldier, Marjorie?"

Marjorie smiled.

"I think I'd better tell you all about it. I've never told anyone else."

"What a splendid game," mused Constance, half to herself, when Marjorie had finished. "Do you—would you—could I be a soldier, too, Marjorie? It would help me. You don't know. There are so many things."

The wistful appeal touched Marjorie.

"Of course you can," she assured. "You'd better come to my house to luncheon to-morrow. You can join the army then and go to the game with me."

"I'm not going to the game." The look of expectancy died out of Constance's face.

"You can't be a soldier if you balk at the first disagreeable thing that comes along," reminded Marjorie, slipping her arm through that of her friend. Constance walked a few steps in stolid silence. She could not make up her mind to watch the playing of the girls whom she felt she hated, even to please Marjorie. It was not until they were about to separate that Marjorie said quietly. "Shall I tell mother you are coming?" and Constance forced herself to reply shortly, "I'll come."

By half past one Saturday afternoon every seat in the large gallery surrounding the gymnasium was filled, and by a quarter to two every square foot of standing room was occupied by an enthusiastic audience largely composed of boys and girls of the two high schools. Marjorie's mother had after some little coaxing consented to come to the game with her daughter as her guest. She sat with Constance and Marjorie in the first row of the gallery, while beside her sat none other than Miss Archer, whom they had encountered on their way to the high school and who had invited them to take seats in the front row with her. She had already met Mrs. Dean at the church which both women attended and had conceived an instant liking for the pretty, gracious woman who looked little older than her daughter.

"Wasn't it nice of Miss Archer to ask us to sit here?" whispered Marjorie in her friend's ear. "We have mother to thank for it. She is so dear that no one can help liking her." Marjorie looked adoring admiration at her mother's clear-cut profile. "Do you suppose anyone will mistake us for faculty?"

Both girls giggled softly at such an improbability.

"I never went to a basketball game before," confessed Constance after a time. "What are those girls over there in the red paper hats and big red bows going to do?"

"Oh, that's the sophomore class. They lead their class in the songs. The green and purple girls are the freshman chorus."

"I didn't even know our class colors were green and purple."

"You didn't! Why, that's the reason you and I wore violets to the dance. Almost every freshman had them."

"Oh, look!" Constance's eyes were fixed upon a tiny purple figure that had just emerged from a side door in the gymnasium and was walking slowly across the big floor. Immediately afterward a door opened on the opposite side and a diminutive scarlet-clad boy flashed forth.

"They are the mascots," explained Marjorie, her gaze on the two children who advanced to the center of the room and gravely shook hands. Then the boy in red announced in a high, clear treble: "Ladies and gentlemen, the noble sophomores!"

The door swung wide and a band of lithe blue figures, bearing a huge letter "S" done in scarlet on the fronts of their blouses, pattered into the gymnasium, amid loud applause.

"The valiant freshmen!" piped the purple-clad youngster.

There was a rush of black-clad girls, with resplendent violet "F's" ornamenting their breasts, another volley of cheers from the audience, then a shrill blast from the referee's whistle rent the air, the teams dropped into their places, the umpire, time-keeper and scorer took their stations, and a tense silence settled over the audience.

The referee balanced the ball. Ellen Seymour and Mignon La Salle gathered themselves for the toss. Up it went. The two players leaped for it. The referee's whistle sounded again. The struggle for basketball honors began.

A jubilant shout swelled from the throats of the watching freshmen and their fans. Mignon had caught the ball. She sent it speeding toward Helen Thornton, who fumbled it, and losing her head, threw it away from, instead of to the basket. An audible sigh of disapproval came from the freshman contingent as they beheld the ball pass into the hands of the sophomores, who scored shortly afterward.

Now that the ball was in their hands the sophomores proceeded to show their friends and opponents a few things about playing. They had the advantage and they kept it. Try as the freshmen might, they could not score. The first unlucky error on the part of Helen Thornton had seemed to turn the tide against them. Toward the close of the first half they managed to score, but all too soon the whistle blew, with the score to in favor of the sophomores.

Their fans went wild with delight and their chorus sang or rather shouted gleefully their pet song, beginning,

"Hail the sophomores, gallant band!

See how bold they take their stand!"

to the tune of "Hail Columbia," coming out noisily on the concluding lines,

"Firm and steadfast shall they be,

Marching on to victory;

As a band of players, they

Shall be conquerors to-day."

The freshmen answered with their song, "The Freshmen's Brave Banner," but they did not sing as spiritedly as they had before the beginning of the game.

"I wonder what Jerry and Irma think," commented Marjorie. Their two chums had been detailed to sing in the freshman chorus, which accounted for their absence from the Dean party.

"Jerry looks awfully cross," returned Constance, scanning the opposite side of the gallery where Jerry was singing lustily, her straight, heavy brows drawn together in a savage scowl.

"There goes the whistle!" Marjorie leaned eagerly forward to see the freshman team come in from the side room which they were using. Her alert eyes noted that Muriel looked sulky, Mignon stormy, Susan Atwell belligerent, Harriet Delaney offended, and that Helen Thornton, the substitute who had replaced her, had been crying.

Marjorie felt a thrill of pity for the unfortunate substitute. It looked as though she had spent an unhappy quarter of an hour in the little side room.

The teams changed sides and hastened to their places. Again Mignon and Ellen faced each other. Then the whistle shrilled and the second half of the game was on.

From the beginning of the second half it looked as though the freshmen might retrieve their early losses. They worked with might and main and made no false moves. Slowly their score climbed to six. So far the sophomores had gained nothing. Then Ellen Seymour made a spectacular throw to the basket and brought her team up two points. With the realization that they were facing defeat the freshmen rallied and made a desperate effort to hold their own, bringing their count up to eight.

Two more points were gained and the score was tied, but the time was growing short. Helen Thornton had the ball and was plainly trying to elude the tantalizing sophomore who barred her way. She made a clumsy feint of throwing the ball. It slipped from her fingers and rolled along the floor. There was a mad scramble for it. Mignon and Ellen Seymour leaped forward simultaneously.

The crowd in the gallery was aroused to the height of excitement. Marjorie, breathless, leaned far over the gallery rail. She knew every detail of the dear old game. She saw Mignon's and Ellen's heads close together as they sprang; then she saw Mignon give a sly, vicious side lunge which threw Ellen almost off her feet. In the instant it took Ellen to recover herself the French girl had seized the ball and was off with it. Eluding her pursuers, she balanced herself on her toes, and threw her prize toward the freshman basket. But it never reached there. A long blue figure shot straight up into the air. Elizabeth Corey, a girl whose sensational plays had made her a lion during her freshman year, had intercepted the flying ball. She sent it spinning through the air toward the sophomore nearest their basket, whose willing hands received it and threw it home.

Mignon's trickery had availed her little. The sophomores had won.

CHAPTER XIV

WHAT HAPPENED ON BLUE MONDAY

For the next ten minutes the air was rent with the lusty voices of the sophomore chorus and the joyous cheers of their fans. No echoing song arose from freshman lips. The vanquished team had already betaken themselves to their quarters, but the sophomore players were holding an impromptu reception on the ground they had so hotly contested.

Marjorie and Constance watched them eagerly.

"Go downstairs, girls, and join the hero worshipers," smiled Miss Archer. "We will excuse you, won't we, Mrs. Dean?"

"Yes; after the fervent manner in which they hung over the railing it would be cruel to keep them with us," smiled Mrs. Dean.

"Let's find Jerry and Irma," said Marjorie, as they paused in the open doorway of the gymnasium.

Hardly had she spoken, when Jerry's unmistakable tones rose behind her. The stout girl was talking excitedly, a rising note of indignation in her voice.

"I tell you I saw her push against Ellen Seymour," she declared. "You must have seen her, too, Irma."

"I thought so," admitted Irma, "but I wasn't sure."

"Well, I was. Oh, girls, we were just going upstairs to find you! Now that you're here, let's go into the gym, and join the celebration. I don't know how you feel about it, but I'm glad the sophomores won," Jerry ended, with an emphatic wag of her head.

"Listen, Jerry," said Marjorie, earnestly, "you were talking so loudly when you were behind us that I couldn't help hearing you. Did it seem to you as though Mignon deliberately pushed against Ellen Seymour?"

"I know she did," reiterated Jerry. "I watched her, for she is always unfair and tricky. Anyone who has ever played on a team could tell. I'm surprised that you——" She stopped abruptly. "I believe you saw her, too. Confess, you did see her; now, didn't you?"

Marjorie nodded.

"Now's your chance to get even with her. Let's go to Miss Archer and tell her," proposed the stout girl. "She'll send for Ellen Seymour and then, good-bye freshman basketball for a while. But what do you care? You aren't on the team any more. It would serve them right at that."

"Oh, no," Marjorie looked her horror at the bare idea of tale-bearing.

"Just as you say," shrugged Jerry. They were still standing just inside the door watching the sophomore team receiving congratulations, when they beheld a familiar figure in a black gymnasium suit pause squarely in front of Ellen Seymour. They saw Ellen start angrily, then a confused murmur of voices arose and the circle of fans and players closed in about the two girls.

"What's happened?" demanded Jerry. "Come on, girls." She hurried toward the crowd, the three girls at her heels. Even as they joined the throng they heard Mignon declare in a tone freighted with malice! "You purposely pushed against me when we ran for the ball in our last play and nearly threw me off my feet. You know that deliberate pushing, striking or any kind of roughness is forbidden, and you could be disqualified as a player. I do not know where the referee's eyes were, I am sure, but I do know that you are not fit to be on a team, and I can prove it by the other players of my team. I shall certainly complain to Miss Archer about it the first thing Monday morning."

"All right, I'll meet you in Miss Archer's office the first thing after chapel," answered Ellen, coolly, ignoring everything save the French girl's final threat. "Come along, girls." She beckoned to the other members of her team, who had listened in blank amazement to the bold accusation. With her head held high, a careless smile on her fine face, Ellen marched through the crowd, which made way for her, and across the gymnasium to the sophomores' room, accompanied by her team.

"Isn't that a shame?" burst out Jerry. "Ellen will have an awful time to prove herself innocent. She never touched Mignon. It was Mignon who pushed her away. I saw her with my own eyes, and so did you, Marjorie. Say," she looked blankly at Marjorie, "do you suppose it's our duty to go to Miss Archer and tell her what we saw?"

"I—don't—know." The words came doubtfully. "Perhaps it will all blow over. I hate to carry tales. Suppose we wait until Monday and see? Mignon may change her mind. Even if she doesn't, Miss Archer may not listen to her. But, if she should, then we'll have to do it, Jerry. It wouldn't be fair to Ellen to keep still about it; I heard Miss Archer tell mother Monday that she would not tolerate the least bit of roughness in the girls' games. She knew of several schools where girls had been tripped or knocked down and seriously hurt. She said that if any reports of rough playing were brought to her she would 'deal severely with the offender.' Those were her very words."

"All right; we'll wait," agreed Jerry. "I'm not crazy about reporting even Mignon. Ellen can take care of herself, I guess."

So the matter was apparently settled for the time, and the four girls strolled home discussing the various features of the game.

"How did you like the game, Captain?" she asked, saluting, as an hour later she entered the living-room, where her mother sat reading.

"Very well, indeed," replied her mother, laying down her magazine. "Neither Miss Archer nor I understand all the fine points of the game, but we managed to keep track of most of the plays. By the way, Marjorie, when you go to school on Monday morning, I wish you to take this magazine to Miss Archer. It contains an article which I have marked for her. It is quite in line with a discussion we had this afternoon."

"I'll remember," promised Marjorie, and when Monday morning came she kept her word, starting for school with the magazine under her arm.

"I'll run up to Miss Archer's office with it after chapel," she decided.

When the morning service was over, Marjorie returned to the study hall, and obtained Miss Merton's grudging permission to execute her commission.

"I wish to see Miss Archer," she said shortly, as Marcia Arnold looked up from her writing just long enough to cast a half insolent glance of inquiry in her direction.

"You can't see her. She's busy."

The color flew to Marjorie's cheeks at the bold refusal. Her first impulse was to turn and walk away. She could see Miss Archer later. Then her natural independence asserted itself, and she determined to stand her ground at least long enough to discover whether or not Miss Archer were really too busy to be seen.

"Then I'll wait here until she is at liberty."

Marcia frowned and seemed on the verge of further unpleasantness when the sound of a buzzer from the inner office sent her hurrying toward it. As she opened the door, Marjorie caught a fleeting glimpse of two persons; one was Miss Archer, her face set and stern, the other Mignon La Salle, her black eyes blazing with satisfaction.

"Oh!" gasped Marjorie, remembering Mignon's threat, "she is reporting poor Ellen."

The door swung open again and the secretary glided past her and out into the corridor with the peculiar sliding gait that had caused Jerry to liken her to a "nice, wriggly snake."

"She is going to bring Ellen here," guessed Marjorie.

Sure enough, within five minutes Marcia returned, followed by Ellen Seymour, whose pale, defiant face meant battle. Again the door of the inner office closed with a portending click. Marcia Arnold did not return to the outer office.

Marjorie waited apprehensively, wondering if Ellen were holding her own. Then to her utter amazement, the secretary appeared with a sulky, "Miss Archer wants you," and returned to her desk.

"Good morning, Miss Dean," was the principal's grave salutation. "I did not know until I asked Miss Arnold to go for you that you were in the outer office."

"I have been waiting to give you the magazine that mother promised you. She asked me to say to you that she had marked the article she wished you to read."

"Please thank your mother for me," returned Miss Archer, her face relaxing, "and thank you for bringing it. To return to why I sent for you, you understand the game of basketball, do you not?"

"Yes," answered Marjorie, simply.

"You have played on a team?" inquired the principal.

"Yes."

"Did I not see you at practice with the freshmen shortly before the game?"

Marjorie colored hotly. "I made the team, but afterward was asked to resign because I did not play well enough."

"Who asked you to resign?"

"The note was signed by the manager of the team."

"And is that the reason you stopped playing?" broke in Ellen Seymour, with impulsive disregard for her surroundings. "I might have known it."

Then she whirled upon Mignon in a burst of indignation as scathing as it was unexpected.

"How contemptible you are! I haven't the least doubt that you are to blame for Miss Dean's leaving the team. You knew her to be a skilful player and you were afraid she would outplay you. You know, too, that when we jumped for the ball Saturday you purposely pushed me away from it, almost throwing me down. It didn't do you the least bit of good, and because you are spiteful you have set out to disgrace me and put a stain on the sophomores' victory."

"How dare you? You are not telling the truth! Prove your charge against me, if you can," challenged Mignon, with blazing eyes.

"It will be easier to prove than yours against me," flung back Ellen.

"Girls, this is disgraceful! Not another word." Miss Archer's tone of stern command had an immediate effect on the belligerents.

"Please pardon me, Miss Archer." There was real contrition in Ellen's voice. "I didn't mean to be so rude. I lost control of my temper."

Mignon, however, made no apology. Her elfish eyes turned from Marjorie to Ellen with an expression of concentrated hate.

"Now, girls," began Miss Archer, firmly, "we are going to settle this difficulty here in my office before anyone of you goes back to her classes. That is the reason I have sent for Miss Dean. When Miss La Salle entered her complaint against you, Miss Seymour, I decided that you should have a chance to speak in your own behalf. No sooner were you brought face to face than one accused the other of treachery. From the front row of the gallery, where I sat on the afternoon of the game, I could see every move of the players, but my eyes were not sufficiently trained to detect the roughness of which you accuse each other. Then I remembered that Miss Dean sat next to me and that she was a seasoned player. So I sent for her to ask her in your presence if she saw the alleged roughness on the part of either of you."

There was a half-smothered exclamation of dismay from Marjorie. Ellen was regarding her in mute appeal. Mignon's lips curled back in a sneer. It was dreadful to remain under a cloud.

"I am waiting for you to speak, Miss Dean."

Marjorie drew a long breath. "Miss Seymour spoke the truth. I saw Miss La Salle purposely push Miss Seymour away from the ball. Someone else saw her, too—someone who sat on the other side of the gallery." Her tones carried unmistakable truth with them.

"It isn't true! It isn't true!" Mignon's voice rose to an enraged shriek. "She only says so because she wants to pay me for making her resign from the team."

"What did I tell you?" asked Ellen Seymour, triumphantly. "She admits that she was responsible for that resignation."

"That will do," commanded Miss Archer, raising her hand.

Ellen subsided meekly.

Realizing that she had said too much, Mignon quieted as suddenly as she had burst forth.

"Miss Dean, are you perfectly sure of what you say?" questioned Miss Archer.

"I am quite sure," was the steady answer.

A seemingly endless silence followed Marjorie's reply. The principal surveyed the trio searchingly.

"What girls comprise the freshman team?" At last she put the question coldly to Mignon.

The French girl sulkily named them. Miss Archer made note of their names. The principal then pressed the buzzer that summoned her secretary.

"Send these young women to me at once," she directed, handing Marcia the slip of paper.

Turning to the three girls before her she said, "Miss Seymour, you may go back to the study hall. Unless you hear from me further you are exonerated from blame. I shall not need you either, Miss Dean. I am sorry that I was obliged to involve you in this affair, but I am glad that you were not afraid to tell the truth."

Marjorie turned to follow Ellen Seymour from the room, when the door opened and the freshman basketball team filed in. For a brief instant the principal's attention was fixed upon the entering girls, and in that instant

Mignon found time to mutter in Marjorie's ear, "I'll never forgive you for this and you'll be sorry. Just wait and see if you're not."

CHAPTER XV

MARJORIE'S WONDERFUL DISCOVERY

What transpired in Miss Archer's private office on that memorable morning when the freshman team visited her in a body was a subject that agitated high school circles for at least a week afterward. Other than the team no one could furnish any authentic information as to what had actually been said and done, but the amazing report that "Miss Archer had disbanded the freshman basketball team" was on every one's tongue. Whether or not another team would be selected no one knew. That would depend wholly upon Miss Archer's decision. That the members of the team had offended seriously there could be no doubt. As for the ex-members themselves, they were absolutely mute on the subject. Among themselves, however, they had a great deal to say, and, one and all, held Marjorie Dean responsible for their downfall.

When Miss Archer had commanded their presence in her office that eventful morning it was not in connection with the conflicting statements of Ellen Seymour and Mignon La Salle. Satisfied that Mignon was the real offender, she had read that young woman a lesson on untruthfulness and treachery in the presence of the team that left her white with mortification, her stormy black eyes alone betraying her rage.

Then Miss Archer proceeded to the other business at hand, which was an inquiry into their reason for requesting Marjorie Dean's resignation from the team. One by one, the four girls, with the exception of Helen Thornton, were questioned separately and acknowledged, in shamefaced fashion, that Marjorie was a really good player.

"Then why," Miss Archer had asked sharply, "did you ask her to resign?" There had been no answer to this pertinent question, and then had followed their principal's rebuke, sharp and stinging.

"It is not often that I feel impelled to interfere in your games," she had said. "Not long since I refused to listen to something Miss Arnold tried to tell me; but, when several heartless girls deliberately combine to humiliate and discomfit a companion under the flimsy pretext of 'the good of the team' it is time to call a halt. Four girls were prime movers in this contemptible plan. One girl was an accessory, and therefore equally guilty. In justice to the traditions of Sanford High School the girl who has suffered at your hands, and in defense of my own self-respect, these offenders must be punished. So I am going to disband your team and forbid any one of you to play basketball again until I am satisfied that you know something of the first principles of honor and fair play. However, I shall not forbid basketball to the freshmen. The innocent shall not suffer with the guilty. A new team will be chosen which I trust will be a credit rather than a detriment to our high school. You are dismissed."

Five girls, whose faces were an open indication of their chagrin, had left the principal's office in a far more chastened frame of mind than when they had entered it. Miss Archer's arraignment had been a most unpleasant surprise, and in discussing it among themselves afterward, Helen Thornton had caused Mignon to pour forth a torrent of biting words by saying sulkily, that if Mignon had let Ellen Seymour alone everything would have been all right.

"Do you mean to say that you believe those miserable girls?" Mignon had cried out.

And Helen had answered with marked sarcasm, "No; I believe what I saw with my own eyes, and I wish I'd never heard of your old team. I'm ashamed to think I ever listened to you," and had walked away from the group with a sore and penitent heart, never to return to their circle again.

All this was, of course, kept strictly secret by the other four ex-members, who joined hands and vowed solemnly that they would weather the gale together. The disbanding of the team by Miss Archer and Ellen Seymour's vindication, could not be hushed up, however, and, despite their protests that Miss Archer was unfair, and that the statements of certain other girls were wholly unreliable, they lost ground with their classmates.

Marjorie, too, had been made to feel the weight of their displeasure, for they took pains to circulate the report that it was she who had told tales to the principal, and thus brought them to grief. Several of the sophomores, including Ellen Seymour, heatedly denied the rumor, and a number of freshmen also took up the cudgels in her behalf. Jerry, Irma and Constance stood firmly by her, and, although the poor little lieutenant was far more hurt over the allegation than she would show, she kept a brave face to the front and tried to ignore the ill-natured thrusts launched chiefly by Muriel and Mignon.

But in the midst of this uncomfortable season Marjorie made a wonderful discovery. It was quite by chance that she made it, and it concerned Constance Stevens. Although the Mary girl had apparently grown very fond of Marjorie and had almost entirely dropped her strange cloak of reserve, she had never invited the girl who had so graciously befriended her to her home.

From the words of vehement protest which Constance had spoken on that day when Marjorie had followed her and protested that they become friends, she had partly understood the other girl's position in regard to her family, and had tactfully avoided the subject ever afterward. She had talked the matter over with her captain, and they had decided to respect Constance's reticence and keep religiously away from anything bordering on the discussion of her family.

It was on a crisp November afternoon, several days before Thanksgiving, that Marjorie made her discovery. As she walked into the living-room, her books on her arm, her cheeks pink from the sharp, frosty air, her mother hung up the telephone with: "Marjorie, do you think Constance would like to go with us to the theatre to-night? Your father has just telephoned me that he has four tickets."

"She'd love it. I know she would. I'll hurry straight down to her house and ask her." Marjorie dropped her books on the table with a joyful thump.

"Very well; but I wish you would wait until I finish my letter, then you can post it on your way there."

"Did Nora bake chocolate cake to-day?" asked Marjorie irrelevantly.

"Yes."

There was a rush of light feet from the room. Three minutes later Marjorie returned, a huge piece of chocolate layer cake in her hand.

"It's the best ever," she declared between bites.

By the time the cake was eaten the letter was ready.

"Hurry, dear," her mother called after her; "we shall have an early dinner."

It did not recur to Marjorie until within sight of the house where Constance lived that she was an uninvited guest. What a queer-looking little house it was! Long ago it had been painted a pale gray with white trimmings, but now it was a dingy, hopeless color that defied description. A child's dilapidated tricycle stood on the rickety porch, which was approached by a flight of three unstable-looking steps.

Her mind centered upon her errand, Marjorie paid small attention to her surroundings. She bounded up the steps, searching with alert eyes for a bell. Finding none she doubled her fist to knock, but paused suddenly with upraised arm. From within the house came the vibrant notes of a violin mingled with the soft accompaniment of a piano.

"Schubert's 'Serenade,'" breathed Marjorie, delightedly, lowering her arm. "I simply must listen."

Suddenly a voice took up the plaintive strain. It was so high and sweet and clear that the listener caught her breath in sheer amazement.

She stood spellbound, while the wonderful voice sang on and on to the last note of the exquisite "Serenade" that seemed to end in a long-drawn sigh.

Marjorie knocked lightly, but no one responded.

The singer had begun again. This time it was Nevin's "Oh That We Two Were Maying."

She listened again; then, to her surprise, the door was gently opened. Before her stood the tiny figure of a boy whose great black eyes looked curiously into hers. Laying his finger upon his lips, he gravely motioned with his other hand for her to enter. Then as he limped away from the door Marjorie saw he was a cripple.

Marjorie stepped noiselessly into the room, her eyes on the piano. A man was seated before it. She could not see his face, but she noted that he had an enormous shock of snow-white hair. At one side of him stood another old man, his thin cheek resting lovingly against his violin, his whole soul intent upon the flood of melody he was bringing forth, while on the other side of the pianist, her quiet face fairly transfigured stood Constance, pouring out her very heart in song.

CHAPTER XVI

THE PEOPLE OF THE LITTLE GRAY HOUSE

Intent upon their music, neither the singer nor the two men were immediately aware of the presence of another person in the room.

"Oh, that we two were lying

Under the churchyard sod,"

sang Constance, voicing the pent-up longing of Kingsley's tenderly regretful words and Nevin's wistful setting, while the violin sang a subdued, pensive obligato.

Marjorie stood very still, her gaze fastened upon Constance. The quaint little boy stared at Marjorie with an equally intent interest. Thus, as Constance began the last line the earnest, compelling regard of the brown eyes caused her own to be turned toward Marjorie.

"Oh!" she ejaculated in faltering surprise. "Where—where did you come from? What made you come here?"

There was mingled amazement, consternation and embarrassment in the question. The white-haired pianist swung round on his stool, and the old man with the violin raised his head and regarded the unexpected visitor out of two mildly inquiring blue eyes.

"I'm sorry," began Marjorie, her cheeks hot with the shame of being unwelcome. "I suppose I ought not to have come, but——"

Constance sprang to her side and catching her hands said contritely, "Forgive me, dear, and please don't feel hurt. I—you see—I never invite anyone here—because—well, just because we are so poor. I thought you wouldn't care to come and so——"

"I've always wanted to come," interrupted Marjorie, eagerly. "I don't think you are poor. I think you are rich to have this wonderful music. I never dreamed you could sing, Constance. What made you keep it a secret?"

"No one ever liked me well enough to care to know it until you came," returned Constance simply. "I meant to tell you, but I kept on putting it off."

While the conversation went on between the two girls the one old man was going over a pile of ragged-edged music on the piano, while the other was industriously engaged with a troublesome E string.

"Father, Uncle John!" called Constance, gently, "come here. I want you to meet my friend Marjorie Dean."

Both musicians left their self-appointed tasks and came forward.

Marjorie gave her soft little hand to each in turn, and they bowed over it with almost old-style courtesy. She looked curiously at Constance's father. His daughter did not in any way resemble him. His was the face of a dreamer, rather thin, with clean-cut features and dark eyes that seemed to see past one and into another world of his own creation. In spite of his white hair he was not old. Not more than forty-five, or, perhaps fifty, Marjorie decided. The other man was much older, sixty at least. He was very thin, and his gentle face wore a pathetically vacant expression that brought back to Marjorie the rush of bitter words Constance had poured forth on the day when she had declined to be friends. "We take care of an old man who people say is crazy, and folks call us Bohemians and gypsies and even vagabonds."

"I came here to see if Constance could go to the theatre with us to-night," explained Marjorie, rather shyly. "No, thank you, I won't sit down. I promised mother I'd hurry home."

"It is very kind in you to ask my daughter to share your pleasure," said Constance's father, his somber face lighting with a smile that reminded Marjorie of the sun suddenly bursting from behind a cloud. "I should like to have her go."

"Have her go," repeated the thin old man, bowing and beaming.

"Is there a band at the theatre?" piped a small, solemn voice.

Marjorie smiled down into the earnest, upraised face of the little boy.

"Oh, yes, there is a big, big band at the theatre."

"Then take me, too," returned the child calmly.

"No, no," reproved Constance gently, "Charlie can't go to-night."

A grieved look crept into the big black eyes. Without further words the quaint little boy limped over to the old man, whom Constance had addressed as Uncle John, and hid behind him.

Forgetting formality, tender-hearted Marjorie sprang after him. She knelt beside him and gathered him into her arms. He made no resistance, merely regarded her with wistful curiosity.

"Listen, dear little man," she said, "you and Constance and I will go to the place where the big band plays some Saturday afternoon, and we'll sit on the front seat where you can see every single thing they do. Won't that be nice?"

The boy nodded and slipped his tiny hand in hers. "I'm going to play in the band when I grow up," he confided. "Connie can go to-night if she promises to tell me all about it afterward."

"You dear little soul," bubbled Marjorie, stroking his thick hair that fell carelessly over his forehead and almost into his bright eyes.

"I'll tell you all about everything, Charlie," promised Constance.

"That means you will go," cried Marjorie, joyfully, rising from the floor, the child's hand still in hers.

"Yes, I will," returned Constance hesitatingly, "only—I—haven't anything pretty to wear."

"Pretty to wear," repeated Uncle John faithfully.

"Never mind that," reassured Marjorie. "Just wear a fresh white blouse with your blue suit. I'm sure that will look nice."

"Will look nice," agreed Uncle John so promptly, that Marjorie started slightly, then, noting that Constance seemed embarrassed, she nodded genially at the old man, who smiled back like a pleased child.

Remembering her mother's injunction, Marjorie took hasty leave of the Stevens family and set off for home at a brisk pace. Her thoughts were as active as her feet. She had seen enough in the last fifteen minutes to furnish ample food for reflection, and she now believed she understood her friend's strange reserve, which at times rose like a wall between them. What strange and yet what utterly delightful people the Stevens were! They really did remind one a little of gypsies. And what a queer room she had been ushered into by the odd little boy named Charlie! She smiled to herself as she contrasted her mother's homelike, yet orderly living-room with the room she had just left, which evidently did duty as a hall, living-room, music-room and also a playroom for little Charlie. There were hats and coats and musical instruments, pile upon pile of well-thumbed music, and numerous dilapidated playthings that bore the marks of too ardent treasuring, all scattered about in reckless confusion. No wonder Constance had fought shy of acquaintanceships which were sure to ripen into schoolgirl visits. Poor Constance! How dreadful it must be to have to keep house, cook the meals and try to go to school! The Stevenses seemed to be very poor in everything except music. She wondered how they lived. Perhaps the two men played in orchestras. Still she had never heard anything about them in school, where news circulated so quickly.

"I'm going to ask Constance to tell me all about it," she decided, as she skipped up the front steps. "Perhaps I can help her in some way."

Constance rang the Deans' bell at exactly half past seven o'clock. Her blue eyes were sparkling with joyous light, and her usually grave mouth broke into little curves of happiness. It was to be a red-letter night for her.

The play was a clean, wholesome drama of American home life in which the leading part was taken by a young girl, who appeared to be scarcely older than Marjorie and Constance. The latter sat like one entranced during the first act, and Marjorie spoke to her twice before she heard.

"Constance," she breathed, "won't you please, please tell me all about it?"

"About what?" counter-questioned the other girl, reddening.

"About your father and your wonderful voice, and, oh, all there is to tell."

"Marjorie," the Mary girl's tones were strained and wistful, "do you really think it is wonderful?"

"You will be a great singer some day," returned Marjorie, simply.

"Oh, do you believe that?" Constance clasped her hands in ecstasy. "I wish to be—I hope to be. If I could only go away to New York city and study! Before we came here we lived in Buffalo. Father played in an orchestra there. He had a friend who taught singing and I studied with him for a year. Then he died suddenly of pneumonia and right after that father fell on an icy pavement and broke his leg. By the time it was well again another man had his place in the orchestra. He had a few pupils, and long before his leg was well he used to sit in a big chair and teach them. The money that they paid him for lessons was all we had to live on."

The rising of the curtain on the second act cut short the narrative. With "I'll tell you the rest later," Constance turned eager eyes toward the stage.

"Isn't it a beautiful play?" she sighed, when the act ended.

"Lovely," agreed Marjorie; "now tell me the rest."

"Oh, there isn't much more to tell. It was the last of March when father got hurt, but it was the middle of May before he was quite well again. Then summer came and most of his pupils went away and we grew poorer and poorer. Just when we were the poorest the editor of a new musical magazine wrote him and asked him to write some articles. A friend of father's in New York told the editor about father and gave him our address. We decided to move to a smaller city, where we could live more cheaply, and some of the musicians that father knew gave him a benefit concert. The money from that helped us to move to Sanford, and father has been writing articles off and on for the magazine ever since then. It's better for all of us to be here. Uncle John isn't quite like other people. When he was a young man he studied to be a virtuoso on the violin. He overworked and had brain fever just before he was to give his first recital. After he got well he never played the same again. He had spent all the money his father left him on his musical education, so he had to find work wherever he could. He played the violin in different orchestras, but he was so absent-minded that he couldn't be trusted. Sometimes he would go on playing after all the rest of the orchestra had finished, and then he began to repeat things after people.

"When father first met him they were playing in the same theatre orchestra. One night a great tragedian was playing 'Hamlet,' and poor Uncle John grew so interested that he said things after him as loud as he could. The actor was dreadfully angry, and so was the leader of the orchestra. He made the poor old man leave the theatre. After that he played in other orchestras a little, but he couldn't be depended upon, so no one wanted to hire him.

"Father did all he could to help him, but he grew queerer and queerer. Then he disappeared, and father didn't see him for a long while. One cold winter night he found him wandering about the streets, so he brought him to his room and he has been with father ever since. That was years ago, before father was married. He isn't really my uncle. I just call him that. The musicians used to call him 'Crazy Johnny.' His name is John Roland."

Although Constance had averred that there wasn't "much to tell," the third act interrupted her recital, and it was during the interval before the beginning of the last act that Marjorie heard the story of the fourth member of the Stevenses' household, little lame Charlie.

"Charlie has been with us a little over four years," returned Constance, in answer to Marjorie's interested questions. "He is seven years old, but you would hardly believe it. His mother died when he was a tiny baby, and his father was a dreadful drunkard. He was a musician, too, a clarionet player. He let Charlie fall downstairs when he was only two years old and hurt his hip. That's why he's lame. His father used to go away and be gone for days and leave the poor baby with his neighbors. Father found out about it and took Charlie away from him, and we've had him with us ever since."

"It was splendid in your father to be so good to the poor old man and Charlie," said Marjorie, warmly.

"Father is the best man in the world," returned Constance, with fond pride. "He is such a wonderful musician, too. He can play on the violin as well as the piano, and he teaches both. If only he could get plenty of work here in Sanford. He has a few pupils, and with the articles he writes we manage to live, but the magazine is a small one and does not pay much for them. He has tried ever so many times to get into the theatre orchestra, but there seems to be no chance for him. I think we'll go somewhere else to live before long. Perhaps to a big city again. I'd love to stay here and go through high school with you, but I am afraid I can't. I'm almost eighteen and I ought to work."

"Oh, you mustn't think of leaving Sanford!" exclaimed Marjorie, in sudden dismay. "What would I do without you? Perhaps things will be brighter after a while. I am sure they will. Why couldn't your father——"

But the last act was on, and she did not finish what had promised to be a suggestion. Nevertheless, a plan had taken shape in her busy mind, which she determined to discuss with her father and mother.

As if to further her design they found Mr. Stevens waiting outside the theatre for his daughter and Marjorie lost no time in presenting him to her father and mother. He greeted the Deans gravely, thanking them for their kindness to his daughter, with a fine courtesy that made a marked impression on them, and after he had gone his way, a happy, smiling Constance beside him, Marjorie slipped her arms in those of her father and mother, and walking between them told Constance's story all over again.

"I think it is positively noble in Mr. Stevens to take care of that old man and little Charlie, when they have no claim upon him," she finished.

"He has a remarkably fine, sensitive face," said Mrs. Dean. "I suppose like nearly all persons of great musical gifts, he lacks the commercial ability to manage his affairs successfully."

"Don't you believe that if the people of Sanford only knew how beautifully Mr. Stevens and the other man played together they might hire them for afternoon teas and little parties and such things?" asked Marjorie, with an earnestness that made her father say teasingly, "Are you going to enlist in his cause as his business manager?"

"You mustn't tease me, General," she reproved. "I'm in dead earnest. I was just thinking to-night that Mr. Stevens ought to have an orchestra of his own. You know mother promised me a party on my birthday, and that's not until January tenth. Why can't I have it the night before Thanksgiving? That will be next Wednesday. Mr. Stevens and Mr. Roland can play for us to dance. A violin and piano will be plenty of music. If everybody likes my orchestra, then someone will be sure to want to hire it for some of the holiday parties. Don't you think that a nice plan?"

"Very," laughed her father. "I see you have an eye to business, Lieutenant."

"You can have your party next week, if you like, dear," agreed Mrs. Dean, who made it a point always to encourage her daughter's generous impulses.

"Then I'll send my invitations to-morrow," exulted Marjorie. "Hurrah for the Stevens orchestra! Long may it wave!" She gave a joyous skip that caused her father to exclaim "Steady!" and her mother to protest against further jolting.

"Beg your pardon, both of you," apologized the frisky lieutenant, giving the arms to which she clung an affectionate squeeze, "but I simply had to rejoice a little. Won't Constance be glad? I could never care quite so much for Constance as I do for Mary, but I like her next best. She's a dear and we're going to be friends as long as we live."

But clouds have an uncomfortable habit of darkening the clearest skies and even sworn friendships are not always timeproof.

CHAPTER XVII

MARJORIE MEETS WITH A LOSS

By eight o'clock the following night twenty-eight invitations to Marjorie Dean's Thanksgiving party were on their way. No one of the invitations ran the risk of being declined. Marjorie had invited only those boys and girls of her acquaintance who were quite likely to come and when the momentous evening arrived they put in twenty-eight joyful appearances and enjoyed the Deans' hospitality to the full.

But to Constance, who wore her beautiful blue gown and went to the party under the protection of her father, whose somber eyes gleamed with a strange new happiness, and old John Roland, whose usually vacant expression had changed to one of inordinate pride, it was, indeed, a night to be remembered by the three. Charlie was to remain at home in the care of a kindly neighbor.

The long living-room had been stripped of everything save the piano, and the polished hardwood floor was ideal to dance on. Uncle John had received careful instructions beforehand from both Mr. Stevens and Constance as to his behavior, and with a sudden flash of reason in his faded eyes had gravely promised to "be good."

He had kept his word, too, and from his station beside the piano he had played like one inspired from the moment his violin sang the first magic strains of the "Blue Danube" until it crooned softly the "Home, Sweet Home" waltz.

The dancers were wholly appreciative of the orchestra, as their coaxing applause for more music after every number testified, and before the evening was over several boys and girls had asked Marjorie if "those dandy musicians" would play for anyone who wanted them.

"Mother's giving a tea next week, and I'm going to tell her about these men," the Crane had informed Marjorie.

"Hal and I are going to give a party before long, and we'll have them, too," Jerry had promised. Lawrence Armitage, who had managed to be found near Constance the greater part of the evening, insisted on being introduced to her father, and during supper, which was served at small tables in the dining-room, he had sat at the same table with the two players and Constance, and kept up an animated and interested discussion on music with Mr. Stevens.

But the crowning moment of the evening had been when, after supper, the guests had gathered in the living-room to do stunts, and Constance had sung Tosti's "Good-bye" and "Thy Blue Eyes," her exquisite voice coming as a bewildering surprise to the assembled young people. How they had crowded around her afterward! How glad Marjorie had been at the success of her plan, and how Mr. Stevens' eyes had shone to hear his daughter praised by her classmates!

In less than a week afterward Constance rose from obscurity to semi-popularity. The story of her singing was noised about through school until it reached even the ears of the girls who had despised her for her poverty. Muriel and Susan had looked absolute amazement when a talkative freshman told the news as she received it from a girl who had attended the party. Mignon, however, was secretly furious at the, to her, unbelievable report that "that beggarly Stevens girl could actually sing." She had never forgiven Constance for refusing to dishonorably assist her in an algebra test, and after her unsuccessful attempt to fasten the disappearance of her bracelet upon Constance she had disliked her with that fierce hatred which the transgressor so often feels for the one he or she has wronged.

Next to Constance in Mignon's black book came Marjorie, who had caused her to lose her proud position of center on the team, and in Miss Merton and Marcia Arnold she had two staunch adherents. Just why Miss Merton disliked Marjorie was hard to say. Perhaps she took violent exception to the girl's gay, gracious manner and love of life, the early years of which she was living so abundantly. At any rate, she never lost an opportunity to harass or annoy the pretty freshman, and it was only by keeping up an eternal vigilance that Marjorie managed to escape constant, nagging reproof.

Last of all, Marcia Arnold had a grievance against Marjorie. She was no longer manager of the freshman team. A disagreeable ten minutes with Miss Archer after the freshman team had been disbanded, on that dreadful day, had been sufficient to deprive her of her office, and arouse her resentment against Marjorie to a fever pitch.

There were still a number of girls in the freshman class who clung to Muriel and Mignon, but they were in the minority. At least two-thirds of — had made friendly overtures not only to Marjorie, but to Constance as well, and as the short December days slipped by, Marjorie began to experience a contentment and peace in her school that she had not felt since leaving dear old Franklin High.

"Everything's going beautifully, Captain," she declared gaily to her mother in answer to the latter's question, as she flashed into the living-room one sunny winter afternoon, with dancing eyes and pink cheeks. "It couldn't be better. I like almost every one in school; Constance's father has more playing than he can do; you bought me that darling collar and cuff set yesterday; I've a long letter from Mary; I've studied all my lessons for to-day, and—oh, yes, we're going to have creamed chicken and lemon meringue pie for dinner. Isn't that enough to make me happy for one day at least?"

"What a jumble of happiness!" laughed her mother.

"Isn't it, though? And now Christmas is almost here. That's another perfectly gigantic happiness," was Marjorie's extravagant comment. "I love Christmas! That reminds me, Mother, you said you would help me play Santa Claus to little Charlie. I don't believe he has ever spent a really jolly Christmas. Of course, Mr. Stevens and Constance will give him things, but he needs a whole lot more presents besides. He climbed into my lap and told me all about what he wanted when I was over there yesterday. I promised to speak to Santa Claus about it. Charlie isn't going to hang up his stocking. He's going to leave a funny little wagon that he drags around for Santa Claus. He told me very solemnly that he knew Santa Claus couldn't fill it, for Connie had said that he never had enough presents to go around, but she was sure he would have a few left when he reached Charlie.

"So Constance and I are going to decorate the wagon with evergreen and hang strings of popcorn on it and fill it full of presents after he goes to bed. He has promised to go very early Christmas eve. Mr. Roland has a little violin he is going to give him, and Mr. Stevens has a cunning chair for him. He has never had a chair of his own. Constance has some picture books and toys, and I'm going to buy some, too. I saved some money from my allowance this month on purpose for this."

Marjorie's face glowed with generous enthusiasm as she talked.

"I am going shopping day after to-morrow," said Mrs. Dean, "and as long as it is Saturday, you had better go with me."

"Oh, splendid!" cried Marjorie, dancing up and down on her tiptoes. "Things are getting interestinger and interestinger."

"Regardless of English," slyly supplemented her mother, as Marjorie danced out of the room to answer the postman's ring.

"Here are two letters for you, Captain, but not even a postcard for me. I'd love to have a letter from Mary, but I haven't answered her last one yet. I'll write to her to-morrow and send her present, too, with special orders not to open it until Christmas."

The next morning Marjorie hurried off to school early, in hopes of seeing Constance before the morning session began. Her friend entered the study hall just as the first bell rang, however, and Marjorie had only time for a word or two in the corridor as they filed off to their respective classes.

"I'll see her in French class," thought Marjorie. "I'll ask Professor Fontaine to let me sit with her." But when she reached the French room and the class gathered, Constance was not among them, nor did she enter the room later. Wondering what had happened, Marjorie reluctantly turned her attention to the advance lesson.

"We weel read this leetle poem togethaire," directed Professor Fontaine, amiably, "but first I shall read eet to you. Eet is called 'Le Papillon,' which means the 'butterfly.'"

Unconsciously, Marjorie's hand strayed to the open neck of her blouse. Then she dropped her hand in dismay. Her butterfly, her pretty talisman, where was it? She remembered wearing it to school that morning, or thought she remembered. Oh, yes, she now recalled that she had pinned it to her coat lapel. It had always shone so bravely against the soft blue broadcloth. She longed to rush downstairs to her locker before reporting in the study hall for dismissal, but remembering how sourly Miss Merton had looked at her only that morning, she decided to possess her soul in patience until the session was dismissed.

Once out of the study hall she dashed downstairs at full speed and hastily opened her locker. As she seized her coat she noted vaguely that Constance's hat and coat were missing, but her mind was centered on her pin. Then an exclamation of grief and dismay escaped her. The lapel was bare of ornament. Her butterfly was gone!

"I wonder if I really did leave it at home?" was her distracted thought, as she climbed the basement stairs with a heavy heart, after having thoroughly examined the locker. But a close search of her room that noon revealed no trace of the missing pin. Hot tears gathered in her eyes, but she brushed them away, muttering: "I won't cry. It isn't lost. It can't be. Oh, my pretty talisman!" She choked back a sob. "I sha'n't tell mother unless it is really hopeless. It won't do any good and she'll feel sorry because I do. It's my own fault. I should have seen that my butterfly was securely fastened."

On the way home from the school that afternoon Marjorie reported the loss of her pin to Irma, Jerry and Constance, who had returned for the afternoon session.

"What a shame!" sympathized Jerry. "It was such a beauty."

"I'm so sorry you lost it," condoled Irma.

"So am I," echoed Constance. "I don't remember it. I'm not very observing about jewelry, but I'm dreadfully sorry just the same."

"It was——" began Marjorie, but a joyful whistle far up the street and the faint ring of running feet put a sudden end to her description. Lawrence Armitage, Hal Macy and the Crane had espied the girls from afar and come with winged feet to join them. Their evident pleasure in the girls' society, coupled with the indescribably funny antics of the Crane, who had apparently appointed himself an amusement committee of one, drove away Marjorie's distress over her loss for the time being, and it was not until later that she remembered that she had not described the butterfly pin to Constance.

CHAPTER XVIII

PLAYING SANTA CLAUS TO CHARLIE

The next morning Marjorie wrote a description of her pin. It was placed at the end of the basement corridor above a small bulletin board, where those who passed might read. She wondered if the loss of her talisman would bring her bad luck. Before the day was over she gloomily decided that it had, for during the last hour Miss Merton accused her of whispering to the girl across the aisle, when she merely leaned forward in her seat to pick up her handkerchief. Smarting with the teacher's injustice, Marjorie politely but steadily contradicted the accusation, and two minutes later found herself on the way to Miss Archer's office, Miss Merton walking grimly beside her.

Miss Archer had been through a particularly trying day, and was irritable, while Miss Merton was consumed with spiteful rage at Marjorie's "impertinence," and did not hesitate to put her side of the story forward in a most unpleasant fashion. The principal turned coldly to Marjory with, "Apologize to Miss Merton at once, Miss Dean, for disturbing her," and Marjorie said, with uplifted chin and resentful eyes, "I am sorry you thought I whispered, Miss Merton, for I did not open my lips." Something in the proud carriage of the girl's head caused Miss Archer to divine the truth of the firm statement, and she said, more gently, "Very well, you are excused, Miss Dean; but I do not wish to hear again that you have failed in courtesy to your teachers. This is not the first time I have received such reports of you."

With a steady, reproachful look at Miss Merton, whose shifting eyes refused to meet hers, Marjorie walked from the room, ready to burst into tears, and when the all but interminable afternoon was ended, hurried home to the shelter of her faithful captain's arms and poured forth her grief and wrongs.

But the notice of the lost pin posted on the bulletin board brought forth no trace of the vanished butterfly. Marjorie made a valiant effort to thrust aside her heavy sense of loss and allow the spirit of Christmas to enter her heart. She had promised Constance her help in arranging Santa Claus' visit to Charlie, and, when on Christmas eve, at a little after seven o'clock she set out for the Stevens' weighed down by numerous festively-wrapped, be-ribboned packages, she was filled with that quiet exaltation that attends the performance of a good deed and happier than she had been for several days.

"Shh!" Constance met her at the door, a warning finger on her lips.

"Hasn't he gone to sleep yet?" asked Marjorie, sliding into the house in mouse-like fashion.

"Yes, but I thought he never would," returned Constance, with a relieved sigh. "What do you think? Father is playing at the theatre to-night for the first time. The pianist is ill. The leader of the orchestra was here this afternoon to see if father would take his place. We can never be grateful enough to you, Marjorie, for having father and Uncle John play at your party."

"Let's talk about Charlie's little wagon," proposed Marjorie, quickly. "Nora popped and strung a lot of corn for me. It's in this bag. Do tell me where I can put the rest of this armful of things."

Constance made a place on one end of an old velvet couch for them.

"This is yours." Marjorie flourished a wide, flat package tied with long, graceful loops of narrow pale blue ribbon. "I tied it with blue because that's your color. Don't you dare peep at it until to-morrow morning. These two little packages are for your father and Mr. Roland, and all the rest is for Charlie."

"He will be the happiest boy in Sanford," said Constance, her own face radiant. "He never dreamed of a Christmas like this."

"Can we begin now?" asked Marjorie. "I'm so impatient to see how this wagon will look when we get it fixed."

"Wait a minute." Constance disappeared through the door leading into the kitchen, returning with one arm piled high with evergreens, the other wound around a small balsam tree.

"Lawrence Armitage brought me this yesterday," she explained. "A party of boys went to the woods to cut down Christmas trees. He brought me this cunning little tree and all this ground pine and holly. Wasn't it nice in him?"

"Perfectly dear," agreed Marjorie. "I wonder if there is enough popcorn for the tree, too. I have a lot of little ornaments and candles at home. It won't take long to go there and back." She reached for her hat and coat as she spoke and in spite of Constance's protests was soon speeding home after the required decorations.

"I made good time, didn't I?" she observed, as half an hour later she burst into the Stevens' living-room without knocking.

Then the work of making one small boy's Christmas merry was begun in earnest. An hour later the sturdy baby balsam stood loaded with its crop of strange fruit, and the faithful, rickety wagon, whose imperfections were quite hidden beneath trails of thick, fragrant ground pine and sprays of flame-berried holly, looked as though it had received a visitation from the fairies. A diminutive black leather violin case, encircled with a wreath of ground pine and tied with a huge red bow, leaned against one wheel of the magic vehicle, and the cunning chair with its absurd little arms and leather cushion was also twined with green.

"It's too lovely for words," breathed Constance, her admiring gaze fastened upon the once dingy corner now bright with the flowers of love and generosity, which had bloomed in all shapes and sizes of packages to gladden one youngster's heart.

"I wish I could be here when first he sees it," commented Marjorie. "I'll be fast asleep then, for he told me that Mr. Roland promised to call him very early."

"He proposed staying up all night, but I was not enthusiastic over that plan," laughed Constance.

"I must go," decided Marjorie. "The hands of that clock fairly fly around the dial. I'm sure I just came and yet they point to a quarter to eleven." She reached reluctantly for her hat and her wraps.

"How can I ever thank you, Marjorie," began Constance, but Marjorie put a soft hand over her friend's lips.

"Please don't," she implored. "I've loved to do it." She held out both hands to Constance. "I wish you the merriest sort of a merry Christmas."

"I hope you will have a perfectly wonderful day," was the earnest response. "You'll come over to-morrow and see how happy you've made Charlie and all of us, won't you?"

"I'll come," promised Marjorie. "You couldn't keep me away."

She reached home just in time to catch a fleeting glimpse of her father disappearing up the stairs with a huge box in his arms, while her mother hastily dropped some thing into the drawer of the library table.

"There, I caught both of you," she cried in triumph. "Confess you were hiding things from me, weren't you?"

"I'll answer your questions to-morrow," beamed her father.

"I forgive you both as long as the things are for me," was her calm declaration.

"What is she talking about?" solemnly asked Mr. Dean, with an air of complete mystification.

"You know perfectly well what I'm talking about!" exclaimed Marjorie, making a rush for him.

"Help, help!" he called feebly. "The battalion has been ambushed and the general captured."

"And held prisoner," added Marjorie, severely. "Unless he informs the second lieutenant what is in a certain big, white box with which he escaped upstairs, he shall be court-martialed."

"Put off the court-martial until to-morrow and perhaps I'll tell," compromised the captured general, throwing his free arm across his lieutenant's shoulder in a most unmilitary manner.

"All right, I'll let you go on parole," returned his daughter. "I'm too sleepy to do guard duty to-night. How I wish you might have seen Charlie's little wagon when we finished it! We had a tree, too."

Forgetting that she was sleepy, Marjorie poured forth the story of her evening's work to her sympathetic listeners and it was ten minutes to twelve before she said good-night and went yawning to bed.

Eight o'clock Christmas morning found her awake and stirring. Wrapped in her bathrobe, she pattered downstairs to the living-room, her arms full of bundles, but her father and mother were already there before her, and their packages greatly outnumbered hers. After the kisses and greetings of the day had been given her father handed the big white box into her outstretched arms. "Shall I tell you——" he began.

"Don't you dare! I'm going to see for myself. Oh-h-h!" She had the lid off, and was clasping to her breast a mass of soft brown fur. "Oh, General, you dear thing! You sha'n't ever go to prison again." She smothered her father in the coat and a rapturous embrace, causing him to protest mildly. Her mother's gift of a bracelet watch also evoked another burst of reckless enthusiasm.

What a happy hour it was, to be sure, and how beautifully all her friends had remembered her! Marjorie could hardly bear to leave her presents long enough to eat breakfast, and when after breakfast she left home for her Christmas call on the Stevens, she felt as though she must sing "Peace on Earth, Good Will Toward Men," at the top of her voice as she walked.

CHAPTER XIX

THE UNLUCKY TALISMAN

There was a rapturous shriek of joy from Charlie as Constance opened the door for Marjorie and their hands and lips met in Christmas greeting. Marjorie stooped to embrace the excited little figure. "Santa Claus did come to see Charlie, didn't he?" she exclaimed, in pretended surprise. "And what did he bring?"

For answer the child limped to his Christmas corner. "Oh, a fiddle," he said reverently, clasping the little violin to his heart. "Now I shall play in the band soon. Johnny said so." He thrust the violin under his sharp little chin, the thin fingers of his left hand reaching across the fingerboard, his left wrist curving into position.

"Why, he holds it like a real violinist!" exclaimed Marjorie. "Can he play?"

Charlie answered her question by dragging his triumphant bow across the helpless strings, drawing forth a wailing discord of tortured sound.

"He thinks he can," giggled Constance. "I suppose those awful sounds are the sweetest music to his ears. Luckily, we don't mind them. I hope you don't. I hate to stop him, he is so delighted with himself."

"I don't mind in the least," assured Marjorie. "I wouldn't spoil his pleasure for anything in the world."

Charlie had no intention of giving a concert that morning, however; he had too many other things to distract his mind.

Marjorie sat on the floor beside the Christmas tree, her feet tucked under her, and listened with becoming gravity and attention while he told her about Santa Claus' visit, and one by one brought forth his precious presents for her to see.

"He must have had enough presents to go around this year or he wouldn't have left me so many," asserted the child with happy positiveness. "Connie's going to write him a letter and say thank you for me. If I don't say 'thank you' when someone gives me something, then I can never play in the band. Johnny and father always say it. I'm sorry I didn't write to Santa Claus before Christmas and ask him for a new leg. I can't go fast on this one. It's been wearing out ever since I was a baby and it keeps on getting shorter."

"Santa Claus can't give you a new leg, Charlie boy," answered Marjorie, her bright face clouding momentarily, "but perhaps some day we can find a good, kind man who will make this poor little leg over like a new one."

"When you find him, you'll be sure to tell him all about me, won't you, Marjorie?" he asked eagerly.

"As sure as anything," nodded Marjory, brushing his heavy black hair out of his eyes and kissing him gently.

"Will you walk down to the drugstore with me, Marjorie?" put in Constance, abruptly.

Marjorie glanced up to meet her friend's troubled gaze. In an instant she was on her feet.

"It's a good thing I didn't take off my hat and coat. I'm ready to go, you see."

"Charlie can watch for us at the window," suggested Constance, hugging the child. "We won't be long."

Once outside the house there was an eloquent silence. "It's dreadful, isn't it?" There was a catch in Constance's voice when finally she spoke.

"Can't he be cured?" queried Marjorie, softly.

"Yes; so a specialist said, if only we had the money."

"He is such a quaint child, and he really and truly believes in Santa Claus," mused Marjorie, aloud. "Most children of his age don't."

"He's different," was the quick reply. "He has been brought up away from other children and in a world of his own. He believes in fairies, too, good ones and bad ones. But he loves music better than anything else in the world, and his highest ambition in life is to play in the band. If only I had the money to make him well! I'd love to see him strong and sturdy like other children."

"You mustn't talk about such sad things to-day, but just be happy," counseled Marjorie, slipping her arm through that of her friend. "Charlie is cheerful and jolly in spite of his poor lame leg. Perhaps the New Year will bring you something glorious."

"You are so comforting, Marjorie," sighed Constance. "I'll throw all my cares to the winds and keep sunny all day if I can."

"I must go now." They entered the little gray house again, just in time to hear remonstrative squeaks from the E string of the diminutive violin, blended with disheartened moans from the A and growls of protest from the G string.

"How did you like that?" inquired Charlie, calmly.

"It was very noisy," criticised Constance.

"It was a very hard passage to play," explained the embryo musician, soberly.

"It seems to have been," laughed Marjorie.

"That is what Johnny says when he doesn't pay attention and makes a mistake on the fiddle," confided Charlie.

Constance's sad look vanished at this naive assertion. "He imitates father and Uncle John in everything," she explained. "He will have played his way through all the music in the house before to-morrow night—most of it upside down, too."

"I'd love to stay longer, but I promised to stop at Macy's and we have our dinner at one o'clock. I wish you could come, too, but I know you'd rather be at home. Thank you again for the hemstitched handkerchiefs. I don't see how you found the time to make them."

"Thank you for the lovely hand-embroidered blouse and all Charlie's things," reminded Constance. "I hope we'll spend many, many more Christmases together."

"So do I," echoed Marjorie, as she kissed Charlie and held out her hand to her friend.

Her call on the Macys lasted the better part of an hour, for Jerry was the recipient of a host of gifts, and insisted upon displaying them, while Hal refused to pose gracefully in the background and absorbed as much of Marjorie's attention as she would give him, secretly wondering if she would be pleased with the box of American Beauty roses he had ordered the florist to deliver at the Deans' residence at noon that day.

What a blissful Christmas it was! From the moment of Marjorie's awakening that morning until the day was done it was one long succession of joyous surprises. And, oh, glorious thought! there were ten blessed days of vacation stretching before her.

"I'll see if Constance will go to the matinee Saturday," she planned drowsily that night as she prepared for sleep. "We will take Charlie. I promised him long ago that I would. I'll run over there to-morrow. Too bad I didn't think of it to-day."

But "to-morrow" brought its own deeds to be done, and so did the following two days, and it was Friday afternoon before Marjorie found time for her visit to the little gray house.

Ever since Christmas it had snowed at intervals and the snow-plow men had been kept busy clearing the streets. It was just the kind of weather to wear one's fur coat, and Marjorie gave a little shiver of delight as she slipped into her Christmas treasure. And how warm it was! The searching east wind that was abroad that day held no discomfort for her.

As she stepped briskly along over the hard-packed walk, hedged in by high-piled snow, she thought rather soberly of her own good fortune and wondered why so many beautiful things had been given to her while to Constance life had grudged all but the barest necessities. With a rush of generous impulse she resolved to do all in her power to smooth the troubled way of her friend.

When within sight of the house Marjorie's eyes were fastened upon the living-room windows for some sign of Charlie, who would sit contentedly at one of them by the hour watching the passersby. Catching sight of his pale little face pressed to the window pane she waved her hand gaily to him. He disappeared from the window and an instant later stood in the open door, shouting gleefully, "Oh, Connie, here's Marjorie! Here's Marjorie!"

Marjorie bent and embraced the gleeful little boy. "How is Charlie to-day?" she asked.

"Pretty well," nodded the child. "I wish I had asked for that leg, though. Mine hurts to-day."

"You poor baby!" consoled Marjorie, tenderly. "But where is Connie, dear?"

"She's upstairs. I'll call her."

He limped across the room to the stair door, which was situated at one side of the living-room, and opened it. "Connie," he called, "Marjorie's come to see us."

There was a sound of quick footsteps on the stairs and Constance appeared. "I didn't know you were here," she apologized.

"Where were you on Thursday?" began Marjorie, laughingly. "You promised to come over. Don't you remember?"

"Yes," returned Constance, briefly. Then with a swift return of the old, chilling reserve, which of late she had seemed to lose, "It was impossible for me to come."

Marjorie scrutinized her friend's face. The look of impassivity had come back to it. "What is the matter, Constance?" she questioned anxiously. "Has anything happened?"

An expression of intense pain leaped into Constance's blue eyes. "I've something to tell you, Marjorie. It's dreadful. I——" With a muffled sob she threw herself, face down, upon the old velvet couch, her slender shoulders shaking with passionate grief.

"Why, Constance!" Marjorie regarded the sobbing girl in sympathetic amazement.

Charlie went over to the couch and patted Constance's fair head. "Don't cry, Connie," he pleaded. Then, limping to a dilapidated writing desk in the corner, which Marjorie never remembered to have seen open before, he took from one of the lower pigeonholes a small, glittering object.

"This is what makes Connie cry." He opened his hand and disclosed a little object on his outstretched palm. "Shall I throw the old thing into the fire, Connie?"

With a sharp ejaculation of dismay, Constance sprang from the couch. One swift glance toward the desk, then she caught Charlie's tiny hand in hers. "Give it to Connie, this minute," she commanded sternly. For the instant Marjorie was forgotten.

Charlie's lips quivered with grieved surprise. Relinquishing his hold on the object he wailed resentfully, "It is a horrid old thing. It made you cry, and me, too."

"Charlie, dear," soothed Constance. Then she glanced up to meet the horrified stare of two accusing brown eyes. "Why—Marjorie!" she exclaimed.

"Where—where—did you get that pin?" Marjorie's soft voice sounded harsh and unnatural.

"That's what I started to tell you," faltered Constance. "Oh, it's so dreadful I can't bear to speak of it. Yet I must tell you. I—the pin——" she broke down and throwing herself on the lounge again began to cry disconsolately.

An appalling silence fell upon the shabby, music-littered room, broken only by Constance's sobs. Marjorie stood rooted to the spot. Could it be true that Constance, the girl she had fought for, the girl for whose sake she had braved class ostracism, had deliberately stolen her pin? Yet she must believe the evidence of her own eyes which had told her that in Charlie's hand lay her cherished pin, her lost, much-mourned-for butterfly!

If Constance had deliberately taken the pin, then she was a thief. If she had found it, but purposely failed to return it, she was still a thief. Marjorie opened her lips to pour forth a torrent of reproaches, but the words would not come. She had a wild desire to pry open the hand which held her precious butterfly and seize it, but her hands remained limply at her sides. It was her pin, her very own, yet she could not touch it unless Constance chose to hand it to her.

But Constance made no such proffer. Still clutching the precious butterfly she continued to weep unrestrainedly.

Marjorie waited patiently.

Having failed hopelessly as a comforter, Charlie had hobbled to his corner, where his Christmas tree still stood, and, with that blessed forgetfulness of sorrow which childhood alone knows, had dragged forth his violin and begun a dismal screeching and scraping, a nerve-racking obligato to his foster sister's sobs.

Five endless minutes passed, but Constance made no sign.

"I'm—I'm going now," choked Marjorie. Hot tears lay thick on her eyelashes. She stumbled blindly toward the door, her face averted from the girl who had so misused and abused her friendship. "Good-bye, Constance."

Something in the reproachful ring of that "Good-bye," startled Constance out of her grief. She had been too greatly overcome with her own trouble to note the effect of her tears and broken words upon Marjorie. Surely Marjorie was not angry with her for crying.

"Wait a minute, Marjorie," she called. "Please don't be angry. I won't cry any more. I want to tell you about the pin. It was——"

But only the sound of a closing door answered her. Marjorie was gone.

CHAPTER XX

THE CROWNING INJURY

Marjorie never remembered just how she reached home that afternoon. She followed the familial streets mechanically, her brain tortured with but one burning thought—Constance was a thief. Over and over the dreadful sentence repeated itself in her mind. "How could she?" was her half-sobbed whisper, as she slipped quietly into the house, and, without glancing toward the living-room, went softly upstairs to her room. She wanted to be alone. Not even her beloved captain could ease the hurt dealt her by the girl she had loved and trusted. Her mother must never know that Constance was unworthy. No one should know, but she could never, never be friends with Constance again.

With the tears running down her cheeks Marjorie took off the new fur coat she had worn so proudly that afternoon and dropped it upon the first convenient chair. Her hat followed it; then throwing herself across the bed, she gave way to uncontrolled weeping. Until that moment she had not realized how greatly she had loved this girl who had Mary's eyes of true blue, but who was so sadly lacking in Mary's fine sense of honor.

Until the afternoon light waned and the shadows began to creep upon her she lay mourning, and inconsolable. Her generous heart had been sorely wounded and she could not easily thrust aside her dreadful sense of loss; neither could she understand why Constance had partly acknowledged that she took the butterfly pin, but had not offered to return it.

"I couldn't ask her for it," she sighed to herself, as, at last, she rose, switched on the electric light, and viewed her tear-swollen face in the mirror, "not when she had kept it all this time. She knew how dreadfully I felt over losing it, and she certainly saw the notice in the hall." A flash of resentment tinged her grief.

"I can't forgive her. I'll never forgive her. I——" Marjorie's lips began to quiver ominously. "I won't cry any more," she asserted stoutly. "My face is a sight now. Mother will ask me what the trouble is, and I don't want a soul to know. Of course, we can't go to the matinee to-morrow. We can't ever go anywhere together again." Once more the tears threatened to fall. She shut her eyes and forced them back, then went dejectedly down the hall to the bathroom to lave her flushed face and aching eyes.

By the time dinner was ready Marjorie showed no traces of her grief. She was unusually quiet at dinner, however, and her mother inquired anxiously if she were ill.

"Did you wear your new coat this afternoon?" her father asked soberly.

"Yes, General. I went to see Constance." Marjorie tried to speak naturally.

"Ah, that accounts for it," he declared, putting on a professional air. "Too much magnificence has struck in. You have, no doubt, a well-developed case of pride and vanity."

"I haven't a single shred of either," protested Marjorie, laughing a little at her father's tone, which was an exact imitation of their former family physician. "That sounded just like good old Doctor Bates."

"Are you and Constance going to take Charlie to the matinee to-morrow, dear?" asked her mother.

"No, Mother," returned Marjorie. Then as though determined to evade further questioning, she asked: "May I go shopping with you?"

"I wish you would. You can select the material for your new dress and the lace for that blouse I am making for you. It is so pretty. My new fashion book came to-day. I have picked out several styles of gowns for you."

"What did you pick out for me?" inquired Mr. Dean, ingenuously.

"You can't have any new clothes. Too much magnificence would strike in. You would have, no doubt, a well-developed case of pride and vanity," retorted Marjorie, wickedly.

"Report at the guard house at once, for disrespectful conduct to your superior officer," ordered Mr. Dean with great severity.

"Not to-night, thank you," bowed the disobedient lieutenant, as all three rose from the table, "I'm going upstairs to my room to write a letter."

Once in her room Marjorie went to her desk and opened it with a reluctance born of the knowledge of a painful task to be performed. Seating herself, she reached for her pen and nibbled the end soberly as she racked her brain for the best way to begin a note to Constance. Finally she decided and wrote:

"Dear Constance:

"I cannot come over to your house to-morrow or ever again. I know what you wanted to tell me. It is too dreadful to think of. You should have told me before. I will never let anyone know, so you need not worry. You have hurt me terribly, and I can't forgive you yet, but I hope I shall some day. I don't like to mention things, but for your own sake won't you try to do what is right about the pin? I shall always speak to you in school, for I don't wish the girls to know we have separated.

"Yours sorrowfully,

"Marjorie."

When she had finished, the all-too-ready tears had again flooded her eyes and dropped unrestrained upon the green blotting pad on her desk. After a little she slowly wiped her eyes, and, without reading what she had written, folded the letter, addressed and stamped it. Slipping into her coat, she wound a silken scarf about her head and went downstairs.

"I'm going out to the mailbox, Mother," she called, as she passed the living-room door.

"Very well," returned Mrs. Dean, abstractedly. She was deep in her book and did not glance up, for which Marjorie was thankful. If her mother noticed her reddened eyelids, explanations would necessarily follow.

The next day dragged interminably. Even the usual pleasure of going shopping with her captain could not mitigate the pain of yesterday's shocking discovery. To Marjorie the bare idea of theft was abhorrent. When, at the Hallowe'en dance, Mignon had accused Constance of taking her bracelet, Marjorie's wrath at the insult to her friend had been righteous and sweeping.

That night, as she sat opposite her mother in the living-room trying to read one of the books she had received for Christmas the incident of the missing bracelet and Mignon's accusation suddenly loomed up in her mind like an unwelcome specter. Suppose Mignon had been right, after all. Jerry had openly asserted that she did not believe Mignon had really lost her bracelet, and in her anger Marjorie had secretly agreed with the stout girl. Suppose Constance had taken it. What if she were one of those persons one reads of in books whom continued poverty had made dishonest, or perhaps she was a kleptomaniac? The last idea, though unpleasant to contemplate, was not so repugnant to her as the first; but she did not believe it to be true. Constance's partial confession, coupled with her ready tears, was positive proof that she had been conscious of her act of theft. There was only one other theory left; she had found the pin and succumbed to the temptation of keeping it. Yet Constance had always averred that she did not care for jewelry, and would not wear it if she possessed it.

Marjorie went over these suppositions again and again, but each time her theories ended with the bitter fact that, in spite of her tears, Constance had kept her ill-gotten bauble.

The vacation which had promised so much, and which she had happily supposed would be all too short, seemed endless. During the long days that followed she received no word from the girl in the little gray house. If Constance had received her letter, she made no sign, and this served to add to Marjorie's belief in her unworthiness.

Jerry Macy's New Year's party proved a welcome relief from the hateful experience through which she had passed. Although invited, Constance was not among the merry gathering of young people, and Jerry loudly lamented the fact. Mr. Stevens and Uncle John Roland, who furnished the music for the dancing, greeted Marjorie with affectionate regard. It was evident that they knew nothing of what had transpired. Constance was ill, her father reported, but hoped to be able to return to school on Tuesday. He thanked Marjorie for her remembrance of him and Charlie, and Uncle John forgot himself and repeated everything after him with grateful nods and smiles.

During the evening Marjorie frequently found herself near the two musicians, and Lawrence Armitage, secretly disappointed because of Constance's absence, also did considerable loitering in their immediate vicinity. If the troubled little lieutenant had had nothing on her mind, she would have spent a most delightful evening, for the Macy's enormous living-room had been transformed into a veritable ballroom, where the guests might dance without bumping elbows at every turn, while Hal and Jerry were the most hospitable entertainers.

If Constance's father and foster uncle had not been present, she might have forgotten her woes, but whenever she glanced at either, the sorrowful face of the Mary girl rose before her. To make matters worse, Jerry proposed to her that they call upon Constance the next day, and Marjorie was obliged to refuse lamely without giving any apparent reason. It was in the nature of a relief to her when the party broke up. In spite of the gratifying knowledge that the girls had pronounced her new white silk frock the prettiest gown of all, and that Hal Macy had been her devoted cavalier, Marjorie Dean went to bed that night in a most unhappy mood.

The Monday before she returned to school she began a long letter to Mary. She and Mary had sworn that, though miles divided them, they would tell each other their secrets. Resolved to keep her word, she had written her heart out to her chum, then had read the letter and torn it into little pieces.

Having written only pleasant things of her new friend to Mary, she could not bear to take away her good name with a few strokes of her pen.

"If only Constance were true and honorable like Mary," she sighed as she closed her desk, and selecting a book she wandered disconsolately downstairs to the living-room to read; but her thoughts continually reverted to her own grievance. "If she gives back my pin, I'll forgive her," was her final conclusion as at last she laid her book aside with an impatient sigh, and sitting down on a little stool near the fire, stared gloomily into its ruddy depths; "but I never, never, never can feel the same toward her again."

Marjorie went to school on Tuesday morning vaguely hoping that Constance would see things in a finer light and act accordingly. Unselfish in most respects, the poor little soldier had forgotten everything save the fact that she was the injured one. To her it seemed as though the other girl's crushing weight of half-acknowledged guilt ought to make her a willing suppliant for pardon. During the early part of the morning session she waited, half expecting to receive a contrite plea for grace from the Mary girl.

When her French hour came, she hurried into the classroom, thinking that she might see Constance before the class gathered; but Professor Fontaine had closed the door and remarked genially, "Bon jour, mesdemoiselles. Comment vous portez vous, aujourd'hui. I trost that you have not forgotten your French during your 'oliday," when it opened quietly to admit Constance.

Marjorie regarded her gravely, noting that she looked pale and tired. Suddenly her eyes opened in wide, unbelieving amazement. With a half-smothered exclamation that caused half the class to turn and look at her, including Mignon, whose alert eyes traveled knowingly between the two girls, she tore her gaze from the disturbing sight, and, putting one hand over her eyes, leaned her head on her arm. For fastened at the open neck of Constance's blouse was her butterfly pin.

CHAPTER XXI

MIGNON PLANS MISCHIEF

To Marjorie, torn between resentment of Constance's bold display of the stolen pin and shame for her utter absence of honor, the French lesson was a confused jumble. She heard but dimly the rise and fall of Professor Fontaine's voice as he conducted the lesson, and when he called upon her to recite she stared at him dazedly and finally managed to stammer that she was not prepared.

"Ah, Mademoiselle Dean, I am of a certainty moch surprised that you cannot translate thees paragraph," the little man declared reproachfully. "I weel begeen eet for you, and you shall do the rest, N'est pas?"

Marjorie stumbled through the paragraph with hot cheeks and a strong desire to throw her book into the air and rush from the recitation. When class was over she seized her books and left the room without looking in Constance's direction.

The eyes of the latter followed her with an expression of perplexed, questioning sorrow that, had Marjorie noted and interpreted as such, might have caused her to doubt what seemed plain, thresh the matter out frankly with Constance, and thus save them both many weeks of misunderstanding and heartache.

At the close of the morning session Marjorie lingered until she was sure that Constance had taken her wraps from the locker and departed. The thought of her beloved pin ornamenting the other girl's blouse was too bitter to be tamely borne. Fierce resentment crowded out her gentler feelings, and she could not trust herself to come in contact with her faithless classmate and remain silent.

On the steps of the school she met Jerry and Irma, who had posted themselves to wait for her.

"I thought you had decided to stay in there all day," grumbled Jerry.

"It's only five minutes past twelve," protested Marjorie.

"I thought it was at least half-past," retorted Jerry. "Say, Marjorie, didn't you say that you'd lost your butterfly pin?"

"Yes," replied Marjorie, shortly, bracing herself for what she felt would follow. She was not the only one who had seen the pin in Constance's possession.

"Did Constance Stevens find it?" quizzed Jerry.

"Yes."

"Oh, then that's all right. I saw her wearing it this morning; and I'm not the only one who saw her, either. Mignon had her eye on it in French class, and I wouldn't be surprised to hear of some hateful remark she had made about it. You know, she still insists that Constance took her bracelet. She might be mean enough to say that Constance found your pin and didn't give it back to you."

Marjorie stared at Jerry in amazement. Without knowing it, the stout girl had exactly stated the truth about the pin.

"You needn't stare at me like that," went on Jerry. "Of course, we know that Constance wouldn't be so silly as to try to keep a pin belonging to someone else that everyone recognized; but lots of girls would believe it. I suppose you let Constance wear it because you two are so chummy; but you'd better get it back and wear it yourself. Then Mignon can't say a word."

"I'll think about it," was Marjorie's evasive answer, but once she had said good-bye to the two girls she began to deliberate within herself as to what she had best do. Here was an exigency against which she had failed to provide. She had resolved never to betray Constance to the girls, but now Constance had, by openly wearing the pin, betrayed herself. Either she would be obliged to go to Constance and demand her own or allow her to wear the bit of jewelry and create the impression that she had sanctioned the wearing of it.

When she returned to school that afternoon she had half determined to see Constance and put the situation fairly to her, but rather to her relief Constance did not appear at the afternoon session, nor was she in school the next day. When Friday came and she was still absent, Marjorie was divided between her pride and a desire to go to the little gray house and settle matters. On Saturday she was still halting between two opinions, and it was four o'clock Saturday afternoon before she put on her wraps with the air of one who has made up her mind and started for the Stevens'.

As she approached the house she looked toward the particular window where Charlie was so fond of stationing himself to peer out on the dingy little street, but there was no sign of the boy's white, eager face. To her vivid imagination the very house itself wore a sad, cheerless aspect that filled her with a vague apprehension of some impending unpleasantness.

She knocked briskly at the door, then waited a little. There was no response. She knocked again, harder and longer, but still silence unbroken by any footfall, reigned within. After pounding upon the door at intervals for at least ten minutes, she turned and walked dejectedly away from the house of denial, speculating as to what could possibly have become of the Stevens'.

At the corner she almost ran against Mr. Stevens, who, with his soft black felt hat pulled low over his forehead, was hurrying along, his violin case under his arm.

"Oh, Mr. Stevens," cried Marjorie, "where is Constance? I have just come from your house, and there is no one at home."

Mr. Stevens looked mildly surprised. "I thought you knew," he answered. "Didn't Constance tell you she was going away? She and Charlie went to New York City yesterday. They are to meet Constance's aunt there. It was very unexpected. She received a letter from her aunt on Tuesday. I was sure she had told you." Mr. Stevens' fine face took on an expression of perplexity.

"I did not know it," responded Marjorie, soberly. "When will she return?"

"I am not quite sure. I shall not know definitely until I hear from her," was the discouraging reply.

"I'm sorry I didn't see her," was all Marjorie could find words for, as she turned to go. "Good-bye, Mr. Stevens."

"Good-bye, Miss Marjorie." The musician bared his head, his thick, white hair ruffling in the wind. "You will hear from Constance, no doubt."

"No doubt I won't," breathed Marjorie, as she walked on. "What would he say, I wonder, if he knew? He'll never know from me, neither will anyone else. I hope those girls will forget all about seeing Constance wear the pin."

But the affair of the pin was destined not to sink into oblivion, for the next morning Marjorie found on her desk the following note:

"Miss Dean:

"Do you think you are doing right in shielding a thief? It looks as though a certain person either stole or found and kept a certain article belonging to you and yet you allow her to wear it before your very eyes without protest. If you do not immediately insist on the return of your property and denounce the thief, we will put the matter before Miss Archer, as this is not the first offense. This is the decision of several indignant students who insist that the girls of the freshman class shall be above reproach."

Marjorie's eyes flashed her contempt of the anonymous missive. She folded it quietly, then, reaching into her desk, drew forth a sheet of note paper and wrote:

"Miss La Salle:

"Although the note I found on my desk is not signed, I am sure that you wrote it. I do not think you have the slightest right to dictate to me in a personal matter. Miss Stevens and I are perfectly capable of settling our own affairs without the help of any member of the freshman class.

"Marjorie Dean."

Mignon's pale face flushed crimson as she read the note which Marjorie lost no time in sending to her via the student route, which was merely the passing of it from desk to desk until it reached its destination. With a scornful lifting of her shoulders she flung the note on her desk, then snatching it up, tore it into tiny pieces.

When school was dismissed she lingered and twenty minutes afterward emerged from Miss Archer's office in company with Marcia Arnold, an expression of triumph in her black eyes.

When she reached home that afternoon she took from the drawer of her dressing-table something small and shining and examined it carefully. "It looks the same, but is it?" she muttered. "Where did the other come from? I don't understand it in the least. Just the same, Marjorie Dean thinks Miss Smarty Stevens took her pin. She was thunderstruck when she saw that Stevens girl wearing it this morning. She's too much afraid of not telling the truth to deny it in her letter. There's something gone wrong with their friendship, too. I'm sure of it from the way they have been acting. I don't know what it's all about, but I do know that this," she touched the small, shining object, "shall never help them solve their problem."

CHAPTER XXII

PLANNING FOR THE MASQUERADE

On the morning following Mignon's visit to Miss Archer's office, Marjorie was unpleasantly startled to hear Miss Merton call out stridently just after opening exercises, "Miss Dean, report to Miss Archer, at once."

A battery of curious eyes was turned in speculation upon Marjorie as she walked the length of the study hall, outwardly composed, but inwardly resentful at Miss Merton's tone, which, to her sensitive ears, bordered on insult.

"Good morning, Miss Archer; Miss Merton said you wished to see me," began Marjorie, quietly, as she entered the outer office where Miss Archer stood, reading a letter which her secretary had just handed to her for inspection.

"Yes," returned the principal, briefly; "come with me." She led the way to her inner office and, motioning to Marjorie to precede her, stepped inside and closed the door.

"Sit here, Miss Dean," she directed, indicating a chair at one side of her desk. Then, seating herself, she turned to the young girl, and said, with kind gravity: "I sent for you this morning because I wish to speak frankly to you of one of your classmates. I shall expect you to be absolutely frank, too. Very grave complaints have been brought to me by Miss La Salle concerning Constance Stevens. She insists that Miss Stevens is guilty of the theft of her bracelet, which disappeared on the night of the dance given by the young men of Weston High School. As I left the gymnasium some time before the party was over, I knew nothing of this, and no word of it was brought to me afterward.

"Miss La Salle also states that Miss Stevens has been wearing a gold pin, in the form of a butterfly, which belongs to you and which you advertised as lost. She declares that she is positive that Miss Stevens found the pin and made no effort to return it to you, and that you are shielding her from the effects of her own wrongdoing by allowing her to continue to wear it. This latter seems to be a rather far-fetched accusation, but Miss La Salle is so insistent in the matter that I was going to settle that part of it, at least, by asking you where and when you found your pin and whether you gave Miss Stevens permission to wear it.

"This may seem to you, my dear, like direct interference in your personal affairs, but it is necessary that this matter be cleared up at once. Miss

Stevens cannot afford to allow such detrimental reports to be circulated about her through the school."

Miss Archer looked expectantly at Marjorie, who was strangely silent, two signals of distress in her brown eyes.

"I cannot answer your questions, Miss Archer," she answered at last, her clear tones a trifle unsteady.

The principal regarded her with amazed displeasure. Accustomed to having the deciding voice in all matters pertaining to her position as head of the school, she could not endure being crossed, particularly by a pupil.

"I must insist upon an answer, Miss Dean. Your silence is unfair, not only to Miss Stevens, but to the school. If Miss Stevens is innocent of any wrongdoing, now is the time to clear her name of suspicion. If she is guilty, by telling the true circumstances concerning your pin, you are doing the school justice. A person who deliberately appropriates that which does not belong to him or to her is a menace to the community in which he or she lives, and should be removed from it. Our school is our community. It must be kept free from those who are a detriment to it," concluded Miss Archer, her mouth settling into lines of obstinate firmness.

The distress in Marjorie's face deepened. "I am sorry, Miss Archer, but I can tell you nothing. Please don't think me stubborn and obstinate. I can't help it. I—I have nothing to say."

"I have explained to you the necessity for perfect frankness on your part, and you have refused to comply with my demand," reproved the principal. "I am deeply disappointed in you, Miss Dean. I looked for better things from you. The affair will have to stand as it is until Miss Stevens returns. I am sorry that you will not assist me in clearing it up." She made a gesture of dismissal. "That is all, I believe, this morning. You may return to the study hall."

Without a word Marjorie rose and left the room, her eyes full of tears, her proud spirit hurt to the quick. The icy reproach in the principal's words was, indeed, hard to bear, and all for a girl who had proved herself unworthy of friendship. Yet she could not help feeling a swift pang of pity for Constance. How dreadful it would be for her when she returned to Sanford and to school!

But Constance seemed in no hurry to return. Midyear, with its burden of examinations, its feverish hopes and fears, came and went. Then followed a three days' vacation, and the new term began with a great readjusting of programs and classes. Marjorie passed her state examinations in American history and physiology, and decided upon physical geography and English history in their places, as both were term studies. She entered upon her second term's work with little enthusiasm, however. The disagreeable, almost tragic events following the holidays had left a shadow on her freshman days, that had promised so much.

February came, smiled deceitfully, froze vindictively, threatened a little, then thawed and froze again, as his next-door neighbor, March, whisked resentfully down upon him, hurried him out of the running for a whole year, and blustered about it for two weeks afterward. The swiftly passing days, however, brought no word or sign concerning the absent Constance, and, try as she might, Marjorie could not forget her.

Mignon La Salle, though greatly disappointed over the failure of her plan to humiliate the musician's daughter, was craftily biding her time, resolved to strike the moment Constance returned to school.

"Mignon certainly intends to make things interesting for Constance," declared Jerry to Marjorie, as the French girl switched haughtily by them one mild afternoon in late March on the way home from school.

"Why do you say that?" asked Marjorie, quickly. "Have you heard anything new?"

"Nothing startling," replied Jerry. "You know Irma and Susan Atwell used to be best friends until they began chumming with Mignon and Muriel. Well, Susan is awfully angry with Mignon for something she said about her, so she has dropped her, and Muriel, too. She went over to Irma's house the other night and cried and said she was sorry she'd been so silly. She wanted to be friends with Irma again."

"What did Irma say?" asked Marjorie, breathlessly.

"Oh, she made up with her, then and there," informed Jerry with fine disgust. "I'd have kept her waiting a while. She deserved it. She told Irma she hoped I'd forgive her, but I didn't make any rash promises."

"What a hard-hearted person you are," smiled Marjorie. "But, tell me, Jerry, what did you hear about Constance?"

"Oh, yes. That's what I started out to tell you. Mignon told Susan last week that she was only waiting for Constance to come back to school to take her to Miss Archer and accuse her of stealing her bracelet."

"How dreadful!" deplored Marjorie. "Perhaps Constance won't come back."

"Yes, she will. She wrote a note to Miss Archer when she went away saying that she had to go to New York City on business, but would return to school as soon as possible. Marcia Arnold saw the note, and told Mignon. Mignon told Susan before they had their fuss. Susan told Irma, and she told me. Almost an endless chain, but not quite," finished Jerry with a cheerful grin.

"I should say so," returned Marjorie, in an abstracted tone. Her thoughts were on the absent girl. She wondered why Constance had gone to New York so suddenly and taken little Charlie with her. She wished she had asked Mr. Stevens more about it.

"See here, Marjorie," Jerry's blunt tones interrupted her musing. "What's the trouble between you and Constance? I know something is the matter, but I'd like most awfully well to know what it is."

"I can't answer your question, Jerry," said Marjorie in a low tone. "Would you care if I—if we didn't talk about Constance?"

"Not a bit," rejoined the stout girl good-naturedly. "Never tell anything you don't want to tell. We'll change the subject. Let's talk about the Sanford High dance. What character do you intend to represent?"

"Is Sanford High going to give a party?" Marjorie voiced her surprise.

"Of course. The Sanford High girls give one every spring, and the Weston boys give their dance in the fall."

"When is it to be?"

"Not until after Easter, and this year it's going to be a lot of fun. We are to have a fairy-tale masquerade."

"I never heard of any such thing before."

"Neither did I," went on Jerry, "that is, until yesterday. The committee just decided upon it. You see, the girls always give a fancy dress party, but not always a masquerade. This year a freshman who was on the committee proposed that it would be a good stunt to make everyone dress as a character in some old fairy tale. The rest of the committee liked the idea, so you had better get busy and hunt up your costume."

"But how did you happen to know so much about it?"

"Well," Jerry looked impressive. "I was on the committee and I happened to be the freshman who proposed it."

"You clever girl!" exclaimed Marjorie, admiringly. "I think that is a splendid idea. I wonder what I could go as?"

"Snow White," suggested Jerry, eyeing her critically. "I can get seven of the Weston boys to do the Seven Little Dwarfs and follow you around."

"But Snow White had 'a skin like snow, cheeks as red as blood and hair as black as ebony,'" quoted Marjorie. "I don't answer to that description."

"You are pretty, and so was she, and that's all you need to care," returned Jerry, calmly. "Besides, the Seven Dwarfs will be great. Will you do it?"

"All right," acquiesced Marjorie. "What are you going as?"

"One of the 'Fat Friars,'" giggled Jerry. "Don't you remember, 'Four Fat Friars Fanning a Fainting Fly'? I'm going to ask three more stout girls to join me. We'll wear long, gray frocks, get bald-headed wigs and carry palmleaf fans. I don't know anyone who would be willing to go as the 'Fainting Fly,' so we'll have to do without him, I guess."

"You funny girl!" laughed Marjorie. "But how will everyone know who is who after the unmasking? There will be so many queens and princesses and kings and courtiers."

"We thought of that and we are going to put up a notice for everyone to carry cards. Some of the characters will be easy to guess without cards."

"I must tell mother about it as soon as I go home and ask her to help me plan Snow White's costume. When will we receive our invitations?"

"We only send printed invitations to the boys. Every girl in high school is invited, of course. The invitations will be sent to the boys next week, and the Sanford girls will be notified at once, so as to give them plenty of time to plan their costumes."

"I wish it were to be next week," murmured Marjorie, after she had left Jerry and turned into her own street. "Everything has been gloomy and horrid for so long. I'd love to have a good time again, just to see how it seemed."

She reflected rather sadly that the disagreeable happenings of her freshman year had outweighed her good times. She had entered Sanford High School with the resolve to like every girl there, and with the hope that the girls would like her, but in some way everything had gone wrong. Perhaps she had been to blame. She had been warned in the beginning not to champion Constance Stevens. Yet the very girls who had warned her could never have been her intimate friends. Her ideals and theirs, if they had ideals, were too widely separated. No; she had been right in standing up for Constance. The fault lay with the latter. It was she who had betrayed friendship.

Determined to go no further into this most painful of subjects, Marjorie resolutely centered her thoughts upon the coming party. The moment she reached home she ran upstairs to her room. Sitting down on the floor before her bookcase, she drew out a thick red volume of Grimms' Fairy Tales and read the story of Snow White. To her joy she discovered that the colored frontispiece was a picture of Snow White begging admittance at the home of the Seven Little Dwarfs.

"I'll ask mother to make me a high-waisted white gown like this one, with pale blue trimmings and a big blue sash," she planned. "I'll wear my pale blue slippers, the ones that have no heels, and white silk stockings. Thank goodness, my hair is curly. I'll let it hang loose on my shoulders. Of course, it isn't as black as ebony; but then, I can't help that." With the book still in her hand she ran down the stairs, two at a time, to tell her mother.

What mother is not interested in her daughter's school fun and parties? Mrs. Dean entered at once into the planning of the costume and suggested that Snow White's cards be made in the shape of little apples, one half colored red, the other half green, and her name written diagonally across the surface of the apple.

Marjorie hailed the idea with delight. "May I buy the water-color paper for the apples to-morrow, Captain?"

"Yes," replied Mrs. Dean. "You ought to begin them at once. What is Constance going to wear? She hasn't been here for a long time. Poor child, I suppose her family keep her busy. Why not ask her to dinner some night this week, Marjorie?"

Marjorie flushed hotly. Her mother, who was busily engaged with an intricate bit of embroidery, did not notice the added color in her daughter's face.

"Constance is in New York visiting her aunt," returned Marjorie. "She has been there for a long time. Charlie is with her. I don't know when they will be home."

Something in her daughter's tone caused Mrs. Dean to glance quickly up from her work. Marjorie was staring out of the window with unseeing eyes.

"Constance has hurt Marjorie's feelings by not writing to her," was Mrs. Dean's thought. Aloud she said: "Did you know before Constance went to New York that she intended going?"

"No; she didn't tell me."

Marjorie volunteered no further information, and Mrs. Dean refrained from asking questions. She thought she understood her daughter's reticence. Marjorie naturally felt that Constance was neglectful and a little ungrateful, but would not say so.

"I wish I could tell mother all about it," ruminated Marjorie, as she went slowly upstairs to replace the Grimms'. "I can't bear to do it. I suppose I shall some day, but it seems too dreadful to say, 'Mother, Constance is a thief. She stole my butterfly pin. That's why she doesn't come here any more.' It's like a disagreeable dream, and I wish I could wake up some day to find that it's all been a dreadful mistake."

But light is sure to follow darkness, and the loyal little lieutenant's awakening was nearer at hand than she could foresee.

CHAPTER XXIII

THE AWAKENING

It was wilful, changeable April's last night, and, being in a tender reminiscent mood, she dispensed her balmiest airs for the benefit of the distinguished company who filled to overflowing the gymnasium of Sanford High School, prepared to dance her last hours away. For the heroes and heroines of fairy-tale renown had apparently left the books that had held them captive for so long, and, jubilant in their unaccustomed freedom, promenaded the floor of the gymnasium in twos, threes or in whole companies.

Simple Simon, whose tall, lank figure bore a startling resemblance to that of the Crane, paraded the floor, calm and unafraid, with none less personage than the terrible Blue Beard. Hansel and Gretel immediately formed a warm attachment for Jack and Jill, and the quartet wandered confidently about together. Little Miss Muffet, in spite of her reputed daintiness, clung to the arm of Bearskin, who, despite the fact that his furry coat was that of a buffalo instead of a bear, was a unique success in his line. One suspected, too that the Brave Little Tailor, whose waistcoat bore the modest inscription, "Seven at One Blow," and who tripped over his long sword at regular two-minute intervals, had an impish, freckled countenance. The straight, lithe figure of the youth with the Magic Fiddle reminded one of Lawrence Armitage, while his constant companion, Aladdin, a sultan of unequaled magnificence, had a peculiar swing to his gait that reminded sharp-eyed observers of Hal Macy. The Four Fat Friars loomed large and gray, and fanned imaginary flies with commendable energy, while Snow White, accompanied by her faithful dwarfs, made a radiantly beautiful figure and was greeted with ejaculations of admiration wherever she chose to walk.

There were kings and courtiers, queens and goose girls. There were jesters and princesses, old witches and fairies. Mother Goose was there. So were Jack Horner, Bo-peep, Little Boy Blue and many more of her nursery children, not to mention two fearsome giants, at least ten feet high, whose voluminous cloaks concealed figures which appeared far too tall to be true. Rapunzel trailed about on the arm of her prince, her beautiful hair, which looked suspiciously like nice new rope, confined in a braid at least three inches wide and hanging gracefully to her feet. Cinderella came to the party in her old kitchen dress, accompanied by her fairy godmother, and Beauty was attended by a strange being clad in a huge fur robe and a papier-mache tiger's head, which was immediately recognized as the formidable Beast.

The gallery of the gymnasium was crowded with the friends and families of the maskers who were admitted by tickets, a limited number of which had been issued. When the first notes of the grand march sounded there was a great craning of necks and a loud buzz of expectation as the gaily dressed company formed into line, and while the brilliant procession circled the gymnasium a lively guessing went on as to who was who in Fairyland.

Mother Goose led the march with the Brave Little Tailor, who frisked along in high glee and executed weird and wonderful steps for the edification of his aged partner and the rest of the company in general.

"Isn't it great, though," commented Aladdin to his partner, who was none other than Snow White. "I know who you are. I'm sure I do. If I guess correctly will you tell me?"

Snow White nodded her curly head.

"All right, here goes. You are Marjorie Dean."

"I'm so glad you guessed right the first time," declared Snow White in a muffled voice from behind her mask. "I've been perfectly crazy to talk to someone. It's a gorgeous party, isn't it, Hal?"

"The nicest one the Sanford girls have ever given the boys," returned Hal Macy, warmly. "You'll give me the next dance, won't you, Marjorie?"

"Of course," acquiesced Marjorie. "I think the grand march is going to end in a minute."

She danced the first dance with Hal. After that the Youth with the Magic Fiddle claimed her, and when he asked in a tone of deep concern, "When do you think Constance will be home, Marjorie?" she had no difficulty in recognizing Lawrence Armitage.

"I don't know, Laurie," she said rather confusedly. "I—I haven't heard from her."

"She wrote me one letter," declared Laurie, gloomily. "I answered it, but she hasn't written me a line since."

"Then you know——" began Marjorie. She did not finish.

"Know what?" asked Laurie, impatiently.

"Nothing," was the answer.

"That's just it!" exclaimed the boy. "I know exactly nothing about Constance. I thought you'd be sure to know something."

Just then the dance came to an end. Jack and the Beanstalk, clad in doublet and hose, and decorated with long green tendrils of that fruitful vine, his famous hatchet slung over his shoulder by a stout leather thong, claimed her for the next dance, and she had no time to exchange further words with Laurie.

The moment of unmasking was to follow the ninth dance. The eighth was just about to begin. Marjorie caught sight of a huge lumbering figure in princely garments heading in her direction, and turning fled toward the dressing-room. She was quite sure of the prince's identity, which was that of a youth whom she particularly disliked. Just as she reached the sheltering door a familiar voice called out a low, cautious, "Marjorie." Turning, she saw a stout, gray-robed friar hurrying toward her.

"I've hunted all over for you," declared the friar, in Jerry's unmistakable tones. "Come into the dressing-room. Someone is waiting to see you there."

"Waiting to see me!" exclaimed Marjorie, in surprise.

"That's what I said. Come along." Jerry caught her arm and pulled her gently into the dressing-room. At one end of the room stood the dingy figure of Cinderella, deep in conversation with her fairy godmother.

At the sound of the opening door Cinderella wheeled and, with a quavering little cry of "Marjorie!" ran forward to meet the newcomers.

Marjorie stopped short and stared unbelievingly at the shabbily clothed figure, but Cinderella had now torn off her mask and was fumbling with trembling eagerness in the pocket of her apron.

"Here it is, Marjorie, dear! I never dreamed you had one like it. No wonder you felt dreadfully that day. Look at it." She thrust a small glittering object into Marjorie's limp hand.

Marjorie regarded the object with a look of growing amazement, which suddenly changed to one of alarm. "It isn't mine!" she gasped. "It's exactly like it except for one thing. Mine has no pearls here." She touched the tips of the golden butterfly's wings. "Oh, Constance, can you ever forgive me?" The pretty butterfly pin slipped from her lax fingers and Marjorie burst into tears.

"Don't cry, Marjorie," said Jerry, with unusual gentleness. "You didn't know. It was just one of those miserable misunderstandings. Constance wants to tell you about the pin."

"But how—where——" quavered Marjorie.

"Oh, I had an idea that there was some kind of a misunderstanding, so I wrote Constance and asked her to come home as soon as she could," explained Jerry. "Her father gave me her address. She was coming home next week, anyhow, but I wrote her again and asked her to get here in time for the dance. The minute I saw that butterfly pin I asked her straight out and out where she got it. She told me, and then I knew that the thing for me to do was to bring you two together. She only came home last night, so we had to plan a costume in a hurry. You haven't said a word about her fairy godmother, either. Take off your mask, dear fairy godmother."

"Irma!" cried Marjorie, as she glimpsed a laughing face. "Oh, it's too wonderful!" She wound two penitent arms around Constance and kissed her.

"I guess that will settle Mignon," commented Jerry, in triumph. "It is a shame, but I suppose your butterfly pin is really lost. Constance will tell you the history of hers."

"I wish the bracelet problem could be solved, too," sighed Constance. "Jerry tells me that Mignon is going to accuse me of taking it when I go back to school. How can she be so cruel? I don't remember seeing it in the dressing-room on the night of the Weston dance."

"But I do!" called out a positive voice that caused them all to face the intruder in astonishment.

A slim, pale-faced girl, dressed as a shepherdess, emerged from behind a curtain which hung in a little alcove at one end of the dressing-room.

"Please excuse me for listening," apologized the girl. "I was standing here looking out of the window when you girls came in and began to talk. Before I could make up my mind what it was all about I heard Miss Stevens talking about Miss La Salle's bracelet and the Weston dance. Did Miss La Salle accuse you of taking her bracelet that night?" she asked, her eyes upon Constance.

"Yes," began Constance, "she——"

"Miss La Salle is the real thief," interrupted the girl, dryly. "I saw her take off her bracelet and lay it on the dressing table. I saw her come and take it away after Miss Stevens left the room. I had to catch the last train home that night. You know, I don't live in Sanford, and I was sitting over in one corner of the dressing-room behind a chair putting on my shoes. Neither Miss Stevens nor Miss La Salle saw me. I wondered what Miss La Salle meant by doing as she did, but I never understood until this minute. I'm glad I happened to be there that night and I'm glad I happen to be here now. If there is likely to be any trouble, just send for me. I'm Edna Halstead, of the junior class."

The four girls had received this rapidly repeated information with varying degrees of amazement. It was Marjorie who first sprang forward and offered her hand to Edna Halstead. "It is the last word we needed to clear Constance," she asserted, joyously. "Will you go to Miss Archer with us on Monday?"

"I should be glad to do so. I never could endure that La Salle girl," was the frank response.

"We'll go together," planned Jerry. "Every one of you meet me in Miss Archer's living-room office on Monday morning before school begins."

"I must go home now," demurred Constance. "I don't wish anyone to know that I've been here."

"Not even Laurie?" asked Marjorie, slyly. "He spoke of you to-night."

Constance smiled. "You may tell him after the 'Home, Sweet Home' waltz."

"There goes the music for the ninth dance," informed Jerry, who had stepped to the door.

"Oh, gracious, I promised this dance to Hal! I can't go. I simply must hear about the pin, Connie."

"I'll tell you just one thing about it," stipulated Constance, "but the rest must wait until to-morrow, for Hal is too nice a boy to leave without a partner."

"Then tell me that one thing," begged Marjorie.

"My aunt sent me the pin," was the quick answer. "Now kiss me good-night and hurry along to Hal."

And Marjorie kissed her and went with happiness singing joyfully in her heart.

CHAPTER XXIV

THE EXPLANATION

Owing to the fervent manner in which each succeeding dance was encored, it was after midnight before the fairy-tale masquerade came to an end and the lords and ladies of fairy lore became everyday boys and girls again; and went home congratulating themselves on the blessed fact that to-morrow was Saturday and that they could make up lost sleep the next morning.

Marjorie Dean, however, was not among the late sleepers. She was up and about the house at her usual hour, for the day held promise of unusual interest. First of all, Constance was coming to see her at ten o'clock. Then too, it was May day, a gloriously sunshiny May day, without the faintest trace of cloud in the deep blue sky. As a third pleasant anticipation, her class had planned a Mayday picnic at a point about two miles up the river. It had been an unusually early spring, and the wild flowers had blossomed in such profusion in the neighboring woods about the town and along the river that the picnic had been planned with a view to spending the day in gathering as many of them as possible.

The expedition having been organized by the officers of the class there was no question of who should be invited or who should be left out. The class was exhorted to turn out in a body, and with the exception of a few girls who had made plans for that Saturday prior to their knowledge of the picnic, the freshmen of — had promised to attend.

"Oh, dear, I wish ten o'clock were here!" sighed Marjorie as she straightened the last object on her dressing table and viewed with satisfaction the immaculate order to which she had reduced her room. Keeping her room clean and dainty was almost a sacred obligation with Marjorie. Her mother had spared neither time nor expense to make it a marvel of pink-and-white beauty. The furniture was of white maple, the thick, soft rug had a cream background scattered with small pink roses. The window curtains were cunning ruffled affairs of fine white dotted Swiss, while the window draperies were in pink-and-white French cretonne. An attractive willow stand, which stood beside the bed, the two pretty willow rockers piled high with pink and white cushions and the creamy wallpaper with its graceful border of pink roses made the room a perpetual joy to its appreciative owner. Marjorie always referred to it as her "house" and when at home spent a great deal of her time there.

But this morning the May sunshine poured rapturously in at her open windows, touched her brown hair with mischievous golden fingers that left gleaming imprints on her curls, and mutely coaxed her to come out and play.

"I can't stand it indoors another minute," she breathed impatiently. "It's almost ten. I'll walk down to the corner. Perhaps I'll see Constance coming."

As she was about to leave the window she caught a glimpse of a slender blue figure far down the street. With a cry of, "Oh, there she is!" Marjorie raced out of her room, down the stairs and across the lawn to the gate.

"You dear thing!" she called, her hands extended.

The next instant the two girls were embracing with a degree of affection known only to those who, after blind misunderstanding, once more see the light.

Tears of contrition stood in Marjorie's eyes as she led Constance into the house and upstairs to her room. "Can you ever forgive me?" she faltered, pushing Constance gently into a chair and drawing her own opposite that of her friend.

"There is nothing to forgive," returned Constance, unsteadily. "You didn't know. If only I had made you stay that day until we came to an understanding! When you said 'Good-bye' in that queer tone, I called to you to wait, for it seemed to me you were angry; but you had gone. Then your note came. I didn't know how you could possibly have learned about the pin, for I hadn't told a soul besides father and Uncle John. It occurred to me that perhaps you had seen Uncle John and he had told you. When I read what you said about not seeing me again I thought just one thing, that, knowing my story, you didn't care to be friends with me any more."

"What do you mean, Constance?" Marjorie's query was full of compelling insistence. "I don't know any story about you."

"I know that you don't, dear; but I thought you knew. When Uncle John came in that afternoon I asked him if he had seen you in the last two days, and he said 'no,' and then 'yes.' I asked him if he had told you about what had happened to me, and he declared that he couldn't remember. I was sure that he had told you, because he often says that when he is afraid father or I won't approve of something he has done. That is the reason I didn't come to see you. Then I went to New York in a hurry without dreaming of what your letter really meant. Jerry wrote me two days before I had planned to come home. So I changed my plans and started for Sanford the same day her letter reached me. Charlie was so much better that I wasn't needed."

"Charlie?" repeated Marjorie, in bewildered interrogation.

"Yes," nodded Constance. "Haven't you seen father since I left? Didn't he tell you?"

"Only once. I—he—I didn't let him know about us. It was right after you went away. He said you had taken Charlie with you. I met him in the street and stopped only a minute. I had come from your house that day but there was no one at home. I couldn't bear to let things go on as they had.

"Now," declared Marjorie, drawing a long breath, "begin at the beginning and tell me every single thing."

"I will," assured Constance, emphatically. "Let me see. It began the day after Christmas. A letter came from New York in the morning mail addressed to father. I gave it to him, and after he read it he sat so still and looked so white that I thought he was going to faint. Then he made me come and sit down beside him and told me that the letter was from my mother's sister in New York and that she was rich and wanted me to come and live with her.

"I said that I would never desert my own father no matter how poor he was, and then he told me that he was only my foster father, just as he was Charlie's. That my own father had been his best friend when they were boys. Later on, my father became a worthless, drunken wretch and my mother had to do sewing to take care of herself and me. My mother's family never forgave her for marrying my father and would not help her. She was not strong and could not stand it to be so poor and work so hard. She died when I was a year old, and just a month afterward my father died with pneumonia. No one wanted me, so I was put in an orphan asylum, but Father Stevens, who had been trying to find my father, heard where I was and took me to live with him. He wrote to my aunt first, but she said she didn't want me. That is the first part of my story."

"It sounds like a story in a book," said Marjorie, softly. "Go on, Connie."

"This letter that father received was from my aunt," continued Constance. "She had been trying to find us for more than two years. Finally, she saw father's name signed to an article in the musical magazine, so she wrote a letter and asked the publishers to forward it. She said in the letter that she was now an old woman who had found that blood was thicker than water, and that she wanted her sister's daughter, who must now be a young woman, to come and live with her. With the letter came a jeweler's box, and in the box was the butterfly pin. She sent it to me as a Christmas gift.

"I cried and said I would not go, but father said it was the opportunity of my life time and that I must. He said that he had no legal right to me and that he loved me too dearly to stand in my way. It almost broke my heart. How I hated that butterfly and my aunt, too. When you came to see me that unlucky day I was feeling the worst. That very night I wrote my aunt a long letter. I told her just how I felt, how much I loved father and Charlie and poor old Uncle John and that I could never, never give them up. Father didn't know I wrote the letter. He thought I was becoming resigned to going away. I went back to school and wore the pin, as my aunt had asked me to do in a little note enclosed in father's letter.

"Then her letter came and it was so much nicer than the other that I cried out of pure happiness. She asked me to bring Charlie to New York. She knew a famous specialist who she thought might help, if not cure him. She asked me to make her a visit and said she would never wish me to come to live with her except of my own free will.

"We went to New York as you know, and, Marjorie"—Constance made an impressive pause—"Charlie is going to be entirely well in a little while. The specialist operated on his hip and the operation was successful. He will be able to walk before very long. When he knew I was coming home he said, 'Tell Marjorie that I don't need to ask Santa Claus for a new leg next year, because the good, kind man she told me about fixed mine.'"

"Dear little Charlie," murmured Marjorie. "I'm so glad."

A pleasant silence fell upon the two young girls. So much had happened that for a brief moment each was busy with her own thoughts.

"Are you coming back to school to finish the year, Constance?" asked Marjorie, at last.

"Yes. I am going to try to make up for lost time. I'll take in June the examinations I should have tried in January. I hope to be a Sanford sophomore, Marjorie. Aunt Edith is coming to visit us this summer. She is going to bring Charlie home."

Constance remained with Marjorie until almost noon.

"I wish you'd stay to luncheon," coaxed the little lieutenant.

"I can't. I'm sorry. I promised father I'd be home at noon."

"Then I wish you were going to the picnic this afternoon."

Constance shook her head, looking wistful, nevertheless.

"I'd rather not. Mignon will be there. It is better to be out of sight and out of mind until after Monday."

"Everything is turning out beautifully," sighed Marjorie. "There's only one thing more that I could possibly wish for."

"What is that?" asked Constance quickly.

"My lost butterfly."

"Perhaps it will fly back home when you least expect it," consoled Constance.

"Lost pins don't fly," retorted Marjorie. "If they did my butterfly would have come back to me long ago."

But, even then, though she could not know it, her cherished butterfly was poising its golden wings for the homeward flight.

CHAPTER XXV

MARJORIE DEAN TO THE RESCUE

By one o'clock that afternoon — had assembled at the big elm tree on the river road which had been chosen as a meeting place. The flower hunters had planned to follow the road for a mile to a point where a boat house, which had a small teashop connected with it, was situated. Owing to the continued spring weather the proprietor had opened the place earlier than usual and it was decided that the picnickers should make this their headquarters, returning there for tea when they grew tired of roaming the neighboring woods.

Marjorie Dean had not hailed the prospect of —'s picnic with enthusiasm. She did not welcome the idea of coming into close contact with the little knot of freshmen that were loyal to Mignon La Salle's interests. However, it would be a pleasure to walk in the fresh spring woods and gather flowers, so she started for the rendezvous that afternoon determined to have the best kind of a time possible under the circumstances.

She had promised to call for Jerry, but the latter, accompanied by Irma, met her halfway between the two houses.

"I thought you were never coming," grumbled the stout girl, in her characteristic fashion.

"I've heard those words before," giggled Marjorie. "Haven't you, Irma?"

"Something very similar," laughed Irma.

Jerry grinned broadly.

"Shouldn't be surprised if you had," she admitted. "It's the first May I ever remember that it hasn't rained. I hope the weather doesn't change its mind and pour before we get home."

"Don't speak of it," cautioned Irma, superstitiously. "You'll bring rain down upon us if you do. May is a weepy month, you know."

"Weeps or no weeps, I suppose we'll have the pleasure of seeing our dear friends, Mignon and Muriel, to-day. I could weep for that," growled Jerry, resentfully.

Arrived at the elm tree, the girls found the majority of their classmates already there. To Marjorie's secret disgust, Marcia Arnold was among the number of upper-class girls chosen to chaperon the picnickers.

"Mignon's work," confided Jerry, as she caught sight of Marcia. "I hope she falls into the river and gets a good wetting," she added, with cheerful malice.

"Jerry!" expostulated Irma in horror. "You mustn't say such awful things."

"I didn't say I hoped she'd get drowned," flung back Jerry. "I'd just like to see her get a good ducking."

It was impossible not to laugh at Jerry, who, encouraged by their laughter, made various other uncomplimentary remarks about the offending junior.

The picnic party set out for the boathouse with merry shouts and echoing laughter. The quiet air rang with the melody of school songs welling from care-free young throats as the crowd of rollicking girls tramped along the river road.

Spring had not been niggardly with her flower wealth, and gracious, smiling May trailed her pink-and-white skirts over carpets of living green, starred with hepaticas and spring beauties, while, from under clusters of green-brown leaves, the trailing arbutus lifted its shy, delicate face to peep out, the loveliest messenger of spring.

The girls pounced upon the fragrant clumps of blossoms and began an enthusiastic filling of baskets. Held captive by the lure of the waking woods, the time slipped by unnoticed, and it was after four o'clock before the majority of the flower-hunters turned their steps toward the boathouse.

Mignon La Salle, Muriel Harding, Marcia Arnold and half a dozen girls who were worshipful admirers of the French girl, soon found flower gathering decidedly monotonous.

"Let's hurry out of these stupid woods," proposed Mignon. "My feet are damp and I'm sure I saw a snake a minute ago."

"Let's go canoeing," proposed Muriel Harding, as they came in sight of the boathouse.

"The very thing," exulted Mignon. "Let me see; there are nine of us. That will be three in a canoe. I'll hire the canoes and tell the man to send the bill to my father."

With quick, catlike springs, she ran lightly down the bank, across the road and disappeared into the boathouse. Ten minutes later three canoes floated on the surface of the river, swollen almost to the banks by April's frequent tearful outbursts. Mignon stood on the shore and gave voluble orders as the girls cautiously took seats in the bobbing craft.

"Get in, Marcia," she commanded, pointing to the third canoe.

Marcia obeyed with nervous expressions of fear.

An hour later, from a little slope just inside the woods, Marjorie and her friends, who had reluctantly directed their steps toward the boathouse, glimpsed the returning canoeing party through the trees. The canoers had lifted their voices in song, and Marcia Arnold, forgetful of her fears, was singing as gaily as the rest.

"It's dangerous to go canoeing now," commented Jerry, judicially. "The river's too high."

"Can you swim?" asked Irma, irrelevantly of Marjorie.

"Yes," nodded Marjorie. "I won a prize at the seashore last year for——"

A sharp, terror-freighted scream rang out. The eyes of the trio were instantly fastened upon the river, where floated an overturned canoe with two girls struggling near it in the water. They saw the one girl strike out for shore, and, unheeding her companions' wild cries, swim steadily toward the river bank.

"Oh!" gasped Marjorie. Then she darted down the slope, scattering the flowers from her basket as she ran. At the river's edge she threw aside her sweater and, sitting down on the ground, tore off her shoes. Poising herself on the bank, she cut the water in a clean, sharp dive and, an instant later, came up not far from Marcia Arnold, who was making desperate efforts to keep afloat.

A few skilful strokes and she had reached the now sinking secretary's side. Slipping her left hand under Marcia's chin, she managed to keep her head above water and support her with her left arm while she struck out strongly for shore with her right. The water was very cold, but the distance was short, and Marjorie felt herself equal to her task.

To the panic-stricken girls on shore it seemed hours, instead of not more than ten minutes, before Marjorie reached the bank with her burden. Willing hands grasped Marcia, who, with unusual presence of mind for one threatened by drowning, had tried to lighten Marjorie's brave effort to rescue her. Once on dry land she dropped back unconscious, while Marjorie clambered ashore, little disturbed by her wetting.

It was Jerry, however, who now rose to the occasion.

"Marjorie Dean," she ordered, "go into that tea shop this minute. I'm going to my house to get you some dry clothes. I'll be back in a little while."

Marjorie allowed herself to be led into the back room of the little shop, where Marcia was already being divested of her wet clothing. Fifteen minutes afterward the two girls sat garbed in voluminous wrappers, belonging to the boat tender's wife, sipping hot tea. Marjorie smiled and talked gaily with her admiring classmates, but Marcia sat white and silent.

Suddenly a girl entered the room and pushed her way through the crowd of girls to Marcia's side. It was Muriel Harding.

"How do you feel, Marcia?" she asked tremulously.

"I'm all right now," quavered Marcia.

Muriel turned impulsively to Marjorie, and bending down, kissed her cheek. "You are a brave, brave girl, Marjorie Dean, and I hope some day I'll be worthy of your friendship." Then she turned and fairly ran from the room.

Before Marjorie could recover from her surprise, Jerry's loud, cheerful tones were heard outside.

"Here's a whole wardrobe," she proclaimed, setting down two suitcases with a flourish. "I came back in our car, and as soon as you girls are dressed, I'll take you home, and as many more as the car will hold," she added genially.

It was a triumphant little procession that marched to the spot where the Macy's huge car stood ready. As Marjorie put her foot on the step a girl's voice called out, "Three cheers for Marjorie Dean!" and the car glided off in the midst of a noisy but heartfelt ovation.

They were well down the road when Marjorie felt a timid hand upon hers. Marcia Arnold's eyes looked penitently into her own. "Will you forgive me, Marjorie?" she said, almost in a whisper. "I've been so hateful."

"Don't ever think of it again," comforted Marjorie, patting the other girl's hand.

"I must think of it," returned Marcia, earnestly. "I—I can't talk about it now, but may I come to see you to-morrow afternoon? I have something to tell you."

"Come by all means," invited Marjorie. "I must say good-bye now. Here we are at my house. I hope mother won't be too much alarmed when I tell her.

I'll have to explain Jerry's clothes. They are not quite a perfect fit, as you can see."

Marcia held the young girl's hand between her own. "I'll come to see you at three o'clock to-morrow afternoon. Maybe I can show you then how deeply I feel what you did for me to-day."

"I wonder what she is so mysterious over," thought Marjorie, as she ran up the steps. "I never dreamed that she and I would be friends. And Muriel, too. How perfectly dear she was. But"—Marjorie stopped short in the middle of the veranda—"what do you suppose became of Mignon?"

CHAPTER XXVI

LETTING BYGONES BE BYGONES

Marjorie touched the button of the electric bell for admittance, but her finger had scarcely left it when the door was opened by her mother, who regarded her daughter with mingled amazement and alarm.

"Why, Marjorie!" she cried. "What has happened to you?"

"Don't be frightened, Mother. I know I look awfully funny!" Marjorie stepped into the hall, with a superb disregard for her strange appearance, assumed with a view to calming Mrs. Dean's fears.

"I—a canoe tipped over and I helped one of the girls out of the river and got wet. My clothes are down at the boathouse drying. Jerry went home and brought back some of hers for me. That's why I look so different. She didn't come here for fear of scaring you."

"You have been in the river!" gasped her mother in horror, "and it's unusually high just now."

"But it didn't hurt me a bit," averred Marjorie, cheerfully. "I can swim, and someone had to help Marcia. Come upstairs with me while I get into my own clothes and I'll tell you all about it."

They had reached her room and Mrs. Dean was eyeing her lively little lieutenant doubtfully. "Are you sure you feel well, Marjorie?" she asked anxiously.

"Perfectly splendid, Captain," was the extravagant assurance, as Marjorie gently backed her mother into a chair. "I'm going to get out of Jerry's clothes and into my own and then we'll have a nice comfy old talk."

Slipping into a one-piece frock of blue linen, Marjorie brushed her dampened brown curls thoroughly dry and let them fall over her shoulders. Placing a sofa pillow on the floor close to her mother, she settled herself cozily at her mother's side and leaned against her knee, looking far more like a little girl than a young woman of seventeen.

It was a very long talk, for there was much to be said, and it lasted until the sun dropped low in the west and the early twilight shadows fell.

A sudden loud ring of the doorbell sent Marjorie scurrying to the door. She opened it to find a messenger boy, bearing a long, white box with the name of Sanford's principal florist upon it.

"For Miss Marjorie Dean," said the boy, handing her the box.

"Oh!" ejaculated the surprised lieutenant, almost dropping the box in her astonishment. Carrying it to the living-room table, she lifted the lid and exclaimed again over its fragrant contents. Exquisite, long-stemmed pink roses had been someone's tribute to Marjorie, and a card tucked in among their perfumed petals proclaimed that someone to be Harold Macy. At the bottom of the card was inscribed in Hal's boyish hand, "To my friend, Marjorie Dean, a real heroine."

Marjorie had scarcely recovered from this pleasant shock when her father appeared upon the scene and gathered her into his arms with an anxious, "How's my brave little lieutenant?"

"Why, General, who told you?" cried Marjorie. "I never dreamed you'd hear of it."

"It came to me through Mr. Arnold, who has the next office to mine," said Mr. Dean. "Mrs. Arnold telephoned him as soon as her daughter reached home. She was afraid he might hear an incorrect report of it from some other source."

"We never thought of that. We should have telephoned you. But it's my fault. I kept mother up in my room and talked so long to her that she forgot it," avowed Marjorie, apologetically.

"It's too late for apologies," Mr. Dean assumed an air of deep injury. Then he laughed and drew from his coat pocket a small package. "Here's an appreciation of bravery," he declared. "To the brave belongs the golden circlet of courage. We might also call it your commission to first lieutenancy. I think you've won your promotion."

Marjorie's second surprise was a gold bracelet, delicately chased, for which she had sighed more than once.

Sunday dawned as radiantly as had the preceding day. Marjorie went to church in a peculiarly exalted mood, and came home feeling at peace with the world. After dinner she took a book and went out into a little vine-covered pagoda built at one end of the lawn, which was fitted with rustic seats and a small table. Here it was that she and her captain had planned to spend many of the long summer afternoons reading and sewing, and it was here that Marcia found her.

"I have something for you, Marjorie," she said in a low voice. Then she opened a little silver mesh bag and drawing forth a small, glittering object handed it to the other girl.

Marjorie's eyes opened wide. With a gurgle of joy she caught the little object and fingered it lovingly. "My very own butterfly! Where in the world did you find it, Marcia?"

"I didn't find it," returned Marcia, huskily.

"Then who did?"

"Mignon. She found it the day after you lost it. I don't like to tell you these things, but I believe it is right that you should know. She kept it merely to hurt you. She knew you were fond of it. Muriel told her all about your receiving it as a farewell gift from your friends. I—I—am to blame, too. I knew she had it. She intended to give it back after a while. Then she saw Miss Stevens with one like it and noticed the queer way you looked at her pin in French class that day. She is very shrewd and observing. She suspected that you girls had quarreled, and so she put two and two together. She actually hates Miss Stevens, and told me she would never give the pin back if she could make Miss Stevens any trouble by keeping it.

"Then she went to Miss Archer and told her about her bracelet and the pin, too." Marcia paused, looking miserable.

"Miss Archer sent for me and questioned me about my pin," said Marjorie, gravely. "She is vexed with me still because I wouldn't say anything. You see I had misjudged Constance. I thought she had found it and kept it. It is only lately that I learned what a dreadful mistake I made. I think I ought to let you know, Marcia, that Constance is in Sanford. She is coming back to school on Monday and going straight to Miss Archer's office to prove her innocence. Constance was Cinderella at the dance Friday night. Jerry made her come to the party on purpose to bring us together. Constance's butterfly pin was a present from her aunt. We know the truth about Mignon's bracelet, too. Did you know that Mignon never lost it, Marcia? She only pretended that she had."

The secretary shook her head in emphatic denial. "I'm not guilty of that, at least. I hope I'll never do anything underhanded or dishonorable again. It's dreadful to think that Miss Archer will have to know what a despicable girl I've been, but that's part of my punishment. I suppose she won't have me for her secretary any more."

Marcia's face wore an expression of complete resignation. She had been a party to a dishonorable act, and her reaping promised to be bitter indeed.

"It means a whole lot to you to be secretary, doesn't it, Marcia?" asked Marjorie, slowly.

"Yes. This is my third year. I've been saving the money to go to college. Father couldn't afford to pay all my expenses. I——" Marcia broke down and covered her face with her hands.

Marjorie regarded the secretary with a puzzled frown. She was apparently turning over some problem in her mind.

"Marcia, how did you obtain my butterfly from Mignon?"

Marcia's hands dropped slowly from her face. "I went to her house this morning and made her give it to me. She tried to make me promise that I would say she found it only a day or two ago. I didn't promise. I'm glad I can say that."

"Would you go with me to her home?" asked Marjorie, abruptly. "I have thought of a way to settle the whole affair without Miss Archer knowing about either of you."

"Oh, if it could only be settled among ourselves!" cried Marcia, clasping her hands. "I'll go with you. She is at home this afternoon, too. I came from her house here."

"Wait just a moment, then, until I run indoors for my hat."

Marjorie walked briskly across the lawn to the house. She was back in a twinkling, a pretty white flower-trimmed hat on her head, carrying a white fluffy parasol that matched her dainty lingerie gown.

"How beautiful Mignon's home is!" she exclaimed softly, as they entered the beautiful grounds of the La Salle estate and walked up the broad driveway bordered with maples. "There's Mignon on the veranda. She is alone. I am glad of that."

"What are you going to say to her?" asked Marcia, her curiosity getting the better of her dejection, for Mignon had risen with a muttered exclamation, and was coming toward them with the quick, catlike movements that so characterized her.

"What do you mean, Marcia Arnold," she began fiercely, "by——"

"Miss Arnold is not responsible for our call this afternoon, Miss La Salle," broke in Marjorie, coolly. "I asked her to come here with me."

Mignon glared at the other girl in speechless anger. Her roving black eyes suddenly spied the butterfly pinned in the lace folds of Marjorie's frock.

"Oh, I see," she sneered. "You think I'm going to tell you all about your trumpery butterfly pin. You are mistaken, I shall tell you nothing."

"I believe I am in possession of all the facts concerning my butterfly," returned Marjorie, dryly, "and also those relating to your supposedly lost bracelet."

"'Supposedly lost?'" repeated Mignon, arching her eyebrows. "Have you found it? If you have, give it to me at once."

"There is only one person who can do that," said Marjorie, gravely, "and that person is you."

The betraying color flew to the French girl's cheeks. "What do you mean?" she asked, but her voice shook.

"Why do you ask me that?" retorted Marjorie, with sudden impatience. "You know that on the night of the Weston dance you pretended you had lost your bracelet in order to throw suspicion on Miss Stevens. Someone saw you lay your bracelet on the dressing table. The same person saw you leave the room, return a few minutes afterward and pick it up from the table. How could you be so cruel and dishonorable?"

"It isn't true," stormed Mignon. "Constance Stevens is a thief. A thief, do you hear? And when she comes back to Sanford the school shall know it."

"No, Constance Stevens is not a thief. You are the real thief," said Marjorie with quiet condemnation. "Knowing the butterfly pin to be mine, you kept it for many weeks. However, I did not come here to quarrel with you. I came to help Marcia and to save you from the effects of your own wrongdoing. Constance Stevens is in Sanford. She is going to Miss Archer to-morrow to prove her innocence. I am going with her. The girl who knows the truth about your bracelet will be there, too. You knew long ago that Constance's butterfly pin was her very own."

"Of course I knew it," sneered Mignon. There was a look of consternation in her eyes, however.

"Then that is another point against you. You do not deserve to be let off so easily, but for Marcia's sake, I am going to say that if you will go with

Constance and me to Miss Archer to-morrow morning and withdraw your charges against Constance, stating that you have your bracelet, we will never mention the subject again. Meet me in Miss Archer's outer office at twenty minutes past eight." She did not even turn to look at the discomfited Mignon as she issued her command.

"Marjorie," said Marcia, hesitatingly, as they walked in silence down the poplar-shaded street. "Shall I—had I—do you wish me to go with you to Miss Archer?"

Marjorie cast a quick, searching glance at the thoroughly repentant junior. "What for?" she smiled, ignoring all that had been. They had now come to where their ways parted. Marjorie held out her hand. "We are going to be friends forever and always, aren't we, Marcia?"

Marcia clasped the extended hand with fervor. "'Forever and always,'" she repeated. And through all their high school days that followed she kept her word.

Three unusually silent young women met in Miss Archer's living-room office the next morning and awaited their opportunity to see the principal.

"Miss Archer will see you," Marcia Arnold informed them after a wait of perhaps five minutes, and the trio filed into the inner office.

"Good morning, girls," greeted Miss Archer, viewing them searchingly. "Miss Stevens, I am glad that you have returned, but I am sorry to say that during your absence I have heard a number of unpleasant rumors concerning you."

Constance flushed, then her color receded, leaving her very white.

Before the principal could continue, Marjorie's earnest tones rang out.

"Miss Archer, Miss Stevens and I had a misunderstanding. When you asked me about it I could not tell you. It has since been cleared away. My butterfly pin has been found, but it was not the one Miss Stevens wore. See, here are the two pins. Mine has no pearls at the tips of the wings." She extended her open palm to the principal. In it lay two butterfly pins, precisely alike save for the pearl-tipped wings of the one.

Miss Archer looked long at the pins. Then she lifted them to meet the blue and the brown eyes whose gaze was fastened earnestly upon her. What she saw seemed to satisfy her. She held out her hand to Marjorie and Constance in turn.

"They are very alike," was her sole comment, as Marjorie returned Constance's pin. Then Miss Archer turned to Mignon.

"I am sorry I accused Miss Stevens of taking my bracelet," murmured Mignon, sulkily. "I have it in my possession. Here it is." She thrust out an unwilling wrist, on which was the bracelet.

"I am glad that you have exonerated Miss Stevens from all suspicion." Miss Archer's quiet face expressed little of what was going on in her mind. "I am also thankful that an apparently serious matter has been so easily settled." She did not offer her hand to Mignon, who left the office without answering.

A moment later, Marjorie and Constance were in the outer office standing at Marcia Arnold's desk. "It's all settled, Marcia, with no names mentioned," she said reassuringly. "Good-bye, we'll see you later. We'll have to hurry or we'll be late for the opening exercises."

In the corridor outside the study hall, Marcia and Constance paused by common consent and faced each other.

"Connie, dear," Marjorie said softly. "There's only a little more than a month of our freshman year left. It isn't very much time, but I believe we won't have to try very hard to make up in happiness for what we've lost."

"I am so happy this morning, and so grateful to you, Marjorie, for all you've done for me, and most of all for your friendship," was Constance's earnest answer. "I hope you will never have cause to question my loyalty and that next year we'll be sophomore chums, tried and true."

"We'll simply have to be," laughed Marjorie, with joyous certainty, "for I don't see how we can very well get along without each other."

THE END